SUNRISE AND SUNSET

Keith Barnes

ARTHUR H. STOCKWELL LTD
Torrs Park, Ilfracombe, Devon, EX34 8BA
Established 1898
www.ahstockwell.co.uk

First published in Great Britain, 1980
Second edition published in Great Britain, 2019

British Library Cataloguing-in-Publication Data.
A catalogue record for this book is available
from the British Library.

ISBN 978-0-7223-4966-3
Printed in Great Britain by
Arthur H. Stockwell Ltd
Torrs Park   Ilfracombe
Devon EX34 8BA

CHAPTER ONE

Prunella thought how apt to be in the garden with a name like hers. Except instead of cutting roses she was loosening the ground underneath the rhododendron bushes with a hoe, intent on extracting weeds, but there were none there. She had in fact decided to do the garden after lunch when assailed by a fit of melancholy, and found unwanted, troublesome and heavy ideas forming. Ideas which she found irreconcilable with the ornate domestic and social routine of her life. She was thirty, unravaged by passion of any kind, and it would be at least another twenty years before the opposite sex would no longer imagine her as a suitable bed mate. So she herself was not a rose which had had its spring and summer, and was waiting for the first October frost. It was in fact the case that no great event was about to shatter her way of life.

Even in small things she received the admiration of everybody who went to the Rotary Club. People felt compelled to congratulate her on the house and garden. Not that she had designed either, but like everyone else she had had a choice, and had chosen perfectly. The rhododendron bushes of mauve and white grew in two ovals cut in the quarter acre lawn, and against a brick wall sweet peas and Michaelmas daisies were only two flowers in a profusion of Victorian hapless horticulture. She had merely insisted when acquiring the house that everything remained as it was. She paid a gardener whose two visits a week ensured that nothing was altered. Built between the two world wars the house had four bedrooms and was perfectly conventional, L-shaped, but not in one respect. The slates were jagged and appeared to be of dissimilar thickness, and many toned, and it was this natural rustic quality which indicated taste.

Inside the house the furniture was neither antique nor modern. Many thought that as they were well-off – her husband had inherited and made money – the items of furniture were made to her specification. They had, however, been acquired already made for little or nothing, and they were the work of craftsmen who had lingered on into the nineteen twenties, and before they disappeared had brought lightness and sparing elegance to heavy Victorian furniture. The framed pictures she had bought for a few shillings each appealed because, although mass-produced, had endeavoured to retain the personal touch of old masters. They represented a world in transition. For example, a stately forecourt which captured the spirit of the times after the uncertainty following the Great War. Also obelisks and love bowers not in an English country park but somewhere else, the location being as far as could be ascertained in Arcadia or somewhere in ancient Greece. Prunella had no desire to go and see the Parthenon. It was simply the charm of the objects which appealed to her. She did not associate them with the last period of craftsmanship, certainly not with Ancient Greece or Aldous Huxley. She liked them as she liked her wedding and engagement rings. One does not repeatedly buy engagement rings, and the garden and the house had the same transitory significance. If a picture broke, or a piece of furniture had woodworm, she would replace them, in the same way as when the fire began to burn low she would either put on some more coal or a log, or turn on the central heating.

The trouble was that her husband and her two children had become to her like the fixtures and fittings. As with these she felt as if she had done what she could and her attention was a matter of convention. Both children, a boy and girl, had been born before she was twenty, and she considered they were now on lines along which, under their own power, they would inexorably move until they married. Really, when she had left them at their first play group she had to all intents and purposes abandoned them: group projects at school, discotheques now, and in time the Young Conservatives or the Young Socialists. As for university, this lay in a nether world because responsibility for them had long disappeared. Her husband as an adult had long ceased to demand any attention. These circumstances, if not typical, were not uncommon. What was uncommon about Prunella, was doing what she did with unintentional style; with elan but with sufficiently unique attitude to have outstanding results, and she would not be choosing fixtures and fittings but getting involved with other people.

So in this vacuum she poked about beneath the rhododendron bushes forgetting all about the non-existent weeds. Reality can be discerned in Turner's paintings; the boats' and ships' forms are not matters for conjecture: at the same time who knows what the inchoate colours which do not paint an actual object indicate. So the objects in Prunella's life were gradually disintegrating and disappearing. She did not go into a trauma, as the reality of life since she had married, her husband, children, house and garden, were swept away like cobwebs. The result was much more prosaic. New shapes, at first indistinct, but after two hours of hoeing assumed definite and precise forms.

That she did not go into a trance, ululate, or become conspicuous in any other way while she hoed does not detract from the emotion of the situation. Her previous mode of life had disappeared, and what may happen subsequently may just assume a superficial difference with the past. She thought about her sexual life, married at seventeen, she thought of groping orgasm and particularly she thought about her present feeling which had moved to one of feeling nothing. Certain meals had to be cooked, and her husband expected her to get into bed naked twice a week. Shortly after getting married he had arrived home after a rugby match boisterous, drunk and singing a song about 'Sally the only girl at the rally'. The chic action to match Sally was to promptly discard her nightdress, and she had been doing so ever since, and now twice weekly.

"I must do something," she said to herself.

By now the ice-cream van which coincided with the children's arrival from school, had been playing its one-line tune.

It was gone half past four and Alison and Robert had passed their mother shouting casually, "Has the gardener left?" It was only after they had entered the house to find no tea ready, and were tugging at their mother's dress that she was shaken out of her reverie. They all went into the house. It was important to the children that the routine when they came home went like clockwork, because by six o'clock when their father Christopher arrived, tea had been eaten and all homework done. No one in the household considered homework seriously for it was assumed that by paying school fees a kind of exemption from the rat race was gained. Success was assured. With a little hustle and bustle tea had been consumed and homework finished just before six, when the financial report on the radio was switched on. Christopher was a stockbroker in the provinces and always expected his wife to give him the closing figures of the Financial Times Index.

"Hello darling. What was the close?" was the usual greeting, repeated today as Christopher came in.

She told him, and he normally never made any comment. She had concluded that the only reason he asked was to assure himself that he was taking life seriously. It might be thought he wasn't a very good stockbroker; money had never bothered them. He had plenty and she had plenty. The only indication of what he thought about finance she had heard from a reply he had given when advice was sought at a party: "Fixed assets, Henry, and a good spread over the rest." She always remembered this, because in matters in which she was not basically interested she liked generalities, conclusions. She was atoise about such matters, but never remembered clichés. She was tolerant of clichés, for three quarters of the people with whom they mixed spoke nothing else. Believing that familiarity does not breed contempt she had a natural tolerance for the artless, humdrum, unspectacular, and those who assiduously read *The Times*, *Telegraph* and *Manchester Guardian* during the day in order to be able to say something in the evening. Christopher encouraged this disinterest she had by arranging his life as orderly as possible. Tonight, for example, they were going to a dinner party for eight, and he required no tea as he had a snack at the office.

That she was a beautiful woman some might think made it unnecessary for her to read the quality papers. Beautiful women, though, make beautiful portraits, but their beauty is no substitute for conversation. Conversation, no matter how banal, is required. Indeed, Prunella's flaxen hair, lightest of brown eyes and skin of white marble drew attention, and some remarks were necessary. Her conversation turned out to be far from banal, and it was completely natural, indiscriminately seeking the peculiar, extraordinary and exquisite in a subject. She was like a magpie collecting trinkets hardly knowing what they were. Practically no one thought her odd, but her languid attitude was probably why she never had an affair. Christopher was thirty-three, three years older then she. Often her questions had an undertone, which although not jarring, hinted, just hinted and so fascinated, at an illiteracy about the ways of the world. Like her garden and her nineteen twenties bric-a-brac, her conversation was unique.

Christopher had two partners. One she asked, would it not be better with inflation to keep money at home, and thus the banks would have less to lend? Not a question that would be put by Professor Galbraithy; of the other one she inquired when the supermarkets were losing so much by pilfering, why assume the stock exchange was morally perfect? Innocent, not disturbing, she was married to Christopher who was a very solid fellow.

Christopher had married her when she was only seventeen and he was twenty. Many who saw her for the first time would think such beauty was allied to great passion, and it was only after closer acquaintance that her languishing manner and esoteric questions made the footloose males in the large provincial town say she dyed her hair, or her eyes were full of lotion and the sparkle not real. Her breasts were always corseted tightly to her body, and marrying young she had done this to show she was no flibbertigibbet but really in love with her husband. This simple action was typical of her, for despite her rather innocent approach to others, she acted so that in one fell swoop she could make her inclinations clear. All the men knew she had breasts likes doves. She had to buy clothes, and this was sufficient to create opinion on the subject which could be covertly relayed from mouth to mouth with that viciousness which characterises secret gossip. Christopher had married her for the very simple reason that this is what she intended. She was self-sufficient, not interested in learning and so in an age when the extraordinary, even one outrageous, sexual relationship was conventional the marriage caused no difficulty, and remained serene until it disappeared during the afternoon when she was hoeing underneath the rhododendron bushes. He was flattered, satiated that such a creature should wish to marry him. For his part he did not know what a love affair was. Of course he realised that people got divorced but if anyone had told him Prunella was having a love affair he would have thought she was buying more of that twenties furniture than the house could hold.

The dinner party had come and gone. The night passed, and after breakfast when Christopher and the two children had departed she was alone. She might just as well have been in Paris or Berlin, Cairo or Samarkand. She felt that her present surroundings were alien, and in the matter of fact attitude, which typified her, her immediate reaction was that she must go on holiday. Holiday venues were soon rejected because they were associated in her mind with her present predicament; Christopher and the children always accompanied her on holidays. She thought of relatives who did not live locally, but relations with these were always of the most formal kind as all had simulated horror at her early marriage. Her mother and father have been omitted because she never even thought of them. They had long disappeared from her life, since they had retired to the Algarve in Portugal to enjoy good weather. She repeated to herself the phrase of the previous day “I must do something", and it became a sort of tranquillizing incantation, and relieved all the immediate tension.

Her mood had been pure feeling after the first obvious means of escape had been scored through and tossed away as impracticable. She now realized it was no use trying to find weeds in a garden that had already been weeded. Her next consideration was to look at the furniture, as she did frequently, for signs of woodworm, but she could not bring herself to do anything so closely associated with her present way of life. If she had gone out of her mind she might have rushed out, got in the car, and driven to some destination where she could assume a fresh identity. If she had merely sought a change or a period in which to sort herself out, the solitude of the Lake District, just up the M6, or the anonymity of London, just down the M1, might have occurred to her. She did not in any way feel tied to her present environment and its habitants, who were her husband and children, the weekly dinner parties of eight – the three partners and their wives and an outsider and his wife – and then the ladies evening at the Rotary, and various sundry activities in which she generally got involved by being married to her husband.

The latter had for many years been events connected with the local Liberal Party, but as her husband was now a Conservative these were events connected with the local Conservative Party. In these she was conspicuous because no one at first knew quite what to make of her, and then decided she was Christopher's wife, and Christopher always spoke and did everything with the greatest discretion and after the most mature consideration. The position of dependence, however, had been achieved by her own feminine insouciance, so really she had a springboard perfectly camouflaged from which someday she might leap into the vortex of circumstances; to say events with regard to Prunella would integrate matters which were dispersed and scattered. Her actions intrigued others, established her position as the wife of her husband, and then seemed to gravitate in an unseen limbo. Such was the result when she wore a yellow and green dress at a Liberal Party function. Nobody had told her, or thought to tell her, that the party colour was now orange. But she was not blamed because everybody took the view that organizations are not perfect, sometimes somebody is not told what they should know. Had her nonchalance, together with her conformity, not been known then she might have been described as reactionary, ostracized, sent to Coventry or hounded out of society, but she had been married ten years and all knew that Christopher's wife was slightly, but only slightly, unpredictable, and in a way that did not disturb any conventions. What had got all this off to a grand start was that at the age of seventeen she had married Christopher without causing gossip even of the most harmless kind. She had looked older, and when her youth became known no one could be found who would criticize young marriages. The reason for acceptance was that after she had decided to marry Christopher she had appeared in the school play. A stranger had asked why in a school with some two hundred and fifty girls had a part been taken by a teacher. He had explained to him that Ophelia was Prunella, who was in the sixth form.

The part established her as a completely independent person in the town. Someone who could make decisions which were safe. A majority of people felt, but never expressed the view, that attached to Shakespeare was an element of mystique. In others the attitude went further. They appeared to themselves like the medieval populace at prayer, only able through a great rood screen occasionally to catch a glimpse of the priest officiating the holy mysteries. Whether or not Shakespeare quirked in the mind, and just jarred it a little, or whether he was viewed with profound vacuity or deep incomprehension, a united attitude coalesced which was delighted and intrigued by the casual manner with which Prunella played Ophelia. She did not know, but had been told that Ophelia was going out of her mind. In the situation thus described, Prunella thought the girl's mental state could be portrayed by confusing the lines; everyone so often declaiming them in the wrong order. There were doubts about whether the great dramatist's text should be so slightly treated. The affair was settled in

Prunella's favour when someone said Hamlet had been played in twentieth century costume, and even rewritten, paraphrased for the uncomprehending. This tour de force on Prunella's part established her in the same category as the teacher producer in the general mind, and so as an adult rather than as an adolescent.

The scenario for the activities of Prunella may be puzzling to those who are not familiar with the intricacy of British life; in this case British life in a large provincial town. The essential characteristic in the way in which at some point one segment is linked to another. It has to be made clear that Prunella and her immediate relatives were not moving about detached from everyone else. A month's careful scrutiny of photographs in the provincial evening paper will see the same faces reappearing at diverse activities.

Having decided that the ground beneath the rhododendron bushes was well and truly tilled, Prunella now relapsed in one gigantic leap to fourteen years before to the one great decision she had made. Normally Prunella didn't make decisions but when she decided to forsake the 'groves of Academe' she had to do so because of parental pressure. For a girl from her stratum of society the progress towards a degree was like taking a horse trained for the Olympics over the fences at some obscure gymkhana at an enlarged vicarage garden party. The house had been built for a local solicitor, and so contained a small room, whose use as a library had been retained. So in here were to be found all the art books, which in a household of this kind are usually deposited somewhere near the television. Her Victorian shriven nineteen-twenties furniture with its slim legs and thin tops, together with the duplicated paintings of some age of the muses and harmony in which an ethereal quality was conveyed by the pleasant decay of some grand portico, but the temporal relevance of which was indicated by robed figures whose costume could not be dated. One of the appealing features of these pictures was the unobtrusive but noticeable finish of their frames, which like all items of this time were never intended to be obsolescent. The first object which met her gaze when she entered the library was their one and only reproduction by a modern artist, Utrillo.

Prunella was not a difficult woman to understand. She liked the particular, the peculiar, the run-of-the-mill if some aspect of it appealed to her. For Christopher, with his ordered business world inherited from his father, she was the ideal wife, part of his 'fixed assets and a good spread'. When he thought about it the furniture was a fixed asset, for it had stood the test of fifty years. Her tastes were modest as far as presents were concerned. Simple strings of jewellery, whose appeal was their cut and colour, perhaps bought by miners at Blackpool for their wives soon after the General Strike. Occasionally little sighs of relief would pass his lips when he thought about the extravagant tastes of the wives of other men all diminishing those 'fixed assets and a good spread' upon which his life was based. When the art books had come flooding in for the children from colleagues at Christmas and birthdays they just couldn't be thrown away, and they couldn't be put alongside the television set for the space was already filled with bric-a-brac. She didn't have any difficulty acquiring vases, brasses, and letter holders from a dealer in town, because she bought what no one else wanted as they were made after the great collectors' divide, the death at the turn of the century of Queen Victoria. To cause no offence she had decided to put a real painting in the library, so that visitors could see that their presents had been noticed. It was of course a reproduction, for 'fixed assets and a good spread' would have been considerably diminished by the acquisition of a real Utrillo. Yet it was acquired quite by chance despite the fact as everyone knows Utrillo with his ability to paint the world as it is, is unique. She knew nothing about movements which Utrillo had withstood, and treated with indifference. She bought it because the narrow street in France with houses on either side from whose upper floor windows the hands of those on the opposite side of the street could be grasped, reminded her of the terraced houses whose occupants had first put on the jewellery she wore. They had postponed having a coloured television set for some time because the colours had not been of the highest quality, and it was Utrillo's loyalty to exactness which had appealed to her. Christopher had readily agreed to the choice because the houses in abundance reminded him of permanence. So although Prunella in closing the library door was seeking an avenue for repose, the painting, because of its associations, reminded her of the vacuum she was seeking to fill.

She sat down and recollected that the decision not to pursue further education was only a strain between her and her parents for the three months it took to commit Christopher to marriage. His father was a stockbroker, and her father was clerk to the council, so how they had both managed to belong to the Young Farmers Club for the moment escaped her, but the rest she remembered with vivid clarity. Because of what she did it must be made clear that subsequently she had always been faithful to Christopher, and she had never been promiscuous. Somehow she had inveigled him into drinking a whole bottle of wine in a lay-by on the way back from a Young Farmers dance. She took his hands so that he did what he would never have done had he been sober, and not in a drunken stupor. She thrust his hand down the front of her dress, and within two days she had convinced him of his power over women in general, and her in particular, and that he had given her great sensual satisfaction, and had only refrained from going as far as possible because he did not wish to take advantage of the fact that she was drunk. Her parents agreed to the match, and A levels ceased to be a topic of conversation. Social life in this provincial town consisted of a constellation with a limited number of stars each of equal brilliance. One of the principal financial advisors or potential financial advisors was definitely a star, and to have married him at the age of seventeen rather than a few years later was considered inconsequential. The social prestige far outweighed any other consideration. It was said, and no doubt quite rightly, that Susan who was taking her French and German very seriously in view of the fact that Britain might join the Common Market, and Jacqueline who was sleeping rough in a hippy commune somewhere in the United Kingdom, would have jumped at the chance.

Why was Prunella so determined not to join the gravy train as it was called now that Latin was slipping out of the syllabus, *gravitas* being the word in Latin for taking matters seriously? She certainly was not averse to free love, then quite popular; neither was she for it. She just considered a university course as unnecessary, and thought that the few eligible men would be further reduced by the time she had her degree. Sitting in the library she was again in the same frame of mind as she had been when deciding on marriage. What she did and what she thought had never required much effort, because she had a certainty of approach which always commended itself to others. Christopher had begun life with her thinking of him as a man whom beautiful women found irresistible, and Prunella was a deluge of a beautiful woman, so now he could concentrate on the business. This quality in one form or another showed itself with everyone with whom she came into contact. The antique dealer in town sold her bric-a-brac that no one else wanted. The gardener, a man in his seventies, found that the old flowers of his youth were the ones she wanted grown. All criticism was initiated by the knowledge of her whole circle that a handmade quilt of innumerable patches and colours covered the marital bed. Everyone thought it was the result of hours, of limitless time, spent, and so she won first prize for it in the local church bazaar. In fact she had completed it on a sewing machine in two afternoons after cutting to bits new clothes and old, quite ruthlessly. Thereafter people were very cautious as to what they asked her to do lest it caused a lot of trouble to someone who was prepared to go to such great lengths to please others. So cautious in fact that she was never asked to do anything else. She had never attended church, deciding in early adolescence that it was unnecessary, but she did not parade her opinion, and the quilt emerged indirectly as a result of her husband's firm agreement that the wife of each partner should support a particular function because it meant fencing for a playground, wasteland that a search in the archives revealed was given to the parson as glebe in the eighteenth century when most open fields disappeared. So proud was everyone that research had revealed the proprietor, that fencing it became a project in which the town assisted the vicar. Equally deep in its effect and repercussions was the quilt which the local newspaper produced on its centre pages in all its variety of colour, grateful to put to good use its newly installed colour printing.

Never at a loss for a facile and adequate solution to any serious problem in the past, Prunella could not imagine what was unnecessary at this present time, a difficulty she had never found herself in before.

Her circle was very limited, and she had no leisure activity regularly which she could incise, cut away from. She was, in this state of affairs, a single animated person among *objet d'art*; people and furniture had become petrified. Because Prunella was unpredictable in what she did, although it might turn out as the acme of convention, it would be impossible to give even the faintest indication as to what would happen. Immersed in the situation, when she had last made a conscious decision of any magnitude, that is when she became determined to marry Christopher, she could see no parallel with present circumstances. So her thoughts emerged from contemplating her young marriage into a void, which for her was a new and startling experience. She had never been at a loss before. It did not occur to her to re-examine that previous event when she had launched on Christopher a sort of blitzkrieg in which she took no time at all in getting him to the marriage bed. She looked around the room, but felt no hostility, no deep-seated animus against that room, or indeed any part of the house or garden, and certainly not towards her husband or children.

Then, as she gazed through the library, she realized that a pair of swallows had a nest under the eaves, and hardly aware of the time, she spent half an hour watching them going out to the garden for food, and then returning. The movement decided her to go shopping in the town, although she required nothing, not even for the weekly dinner party at which she and

Christopher were the hosts this week. As she walked across the length of the library she was aware of the few books on every conceivable topic, bought by Christopher, not for himself but for the children. He had been so impressed by one guest at a dinner party who described himself as a self-made man, that he had determined on building up a collection. He thought some compensatory factor was desired in view of the extraordinary spectacle of the children being sent abroad by their school to improve their French even before the grammatic rudiments of that language had been attempted. Prunella recollected why the books were there, and thought how sensible her husband was and compared him with the nest she had just been looking at and thought how fortunate it was that the saliva of the swallows had a sticky quality, otherwise their curved mud nest would have fallen apart.

She herself, since the age of fourteen, had thought books silly after reading George Eliot's *Adam Bede* in class. Pregnant girls were such a topic of conversation in the school, that while she was there the significance of the town birth rate amongst these uniformed adolescents dropped below the quality of school meals as gossip. How ridiculous it was to have to wait until almost the last page for pregnancy in Eliot's novel. After expressing her view in an essay she was reprimanded for not recognizing unmarried mothers, now and at the time of Eliot, required to be looked at differently. To counter the argument of authority Prunella replied that Marie Antoinette had told people to eat cake, and the aristocracy had always done as they pleased. A final onslaught to illustrate her thoughts was to mention Oliver Goldsmith's *She Stoops to Conquer* then performed as the annual school play. It was of course of an earlier period than Eliot's book, and as the gentry seemed to regard serving maids as belonging to some sort of disseminated brothel for their dalliance, Prunella said as much. The fact that Goldsmith lived before Eliot perfected her notion that genteel whoring was as old as Stonehenge. So she was sceptical and unbelieving about books. The argument spilled over after a parents' evening at the town clerk's home.

All her father wanted her to do then was to remain at school. His participation was completely superfluous, but he wanted her to take her studies seriously and as she seemed quite self-contained and confident about her views, racked his brains and at last fastened on Restoration plays which he pointed out supported the view she had taken. Some sort of empirical confirmation was thought necessary, so Grandfather, who now lived above the Liberal Club after years as agent for a former MP, was brought in to add experience to the debate.

He heard the whole story and simply said to his granddaughter, "You are quite right, my dear."

It was not surprising that after all the furore Prunella remembered the incident.

The silliness of books had been confirmed in her mind five years ago at the time the grand patchwork quilt had appeared at the bazaar. It had led to the vicar being invited to one of the weekly dinner parties. He was a scholarly man en route from the chaplaincy of an Oxford college to a bishopric and was sojourning in the town so the decencies of time could be observed before his elevation. He spoke as a scholar, and began talking about Eliot.

A long silence followed his disquisition as nobody had the remotest notion of what he was talking about. In some circles it is the custom to keep on talking no matter how profound the incoherence which develops, and it is especially the case in these circles for the juxtaposition of words to be maintained in an interminable line although the result lacks sense and meaning. The stockbrokers and their wives might talk in platitudes and clichés, but an eavesdropper could follow what they said. The vicar's monologue complete, if he didn't expect comprehension he would at least get nonsense. No one was quite sure at first whether he had finished, or was just pausing to regain his breath. As the silence lengthened it became obvious it was not the latter. At this point Christopher, who had never known his wife find anything difficult, gave her a quizzical look which she interpreted as calling upon her to say something, which she did.

"Very interesting, vicar, I have always thought *Adam Bede* a silly book."

She had caught the word Eliot, and although not paying much attention had a vague impression that the vicar was telling some sort of funny joke, but decided that it was a kind that could only be understood by other vicars. She was surprised that the others could find nothing to say, for she supposed the clergy required financial advice the same as other people, and also thought that during any colloquy mutual ground for conversation would appear as well-worn furrows. Therefore she had made no attempts to follow what had been said although she had heard the vicar repeat the name Eliot frequently.

Her remark was treated as feigned feminine innocence. His experience of pretty witless females was adequate if not extensive. He had known the charming daughter of the occupant of the see of Oswenfell and Hailness until at the age of nineteen she had disappeared from the Cathedral Close after appearing in widely circulated girlie magazines. Prunella, although pretty, was not witless, but it was fortunate for his fellow diners that he placed her in this category. He regarded her remark as perfect repartee which indicated that he had become the life and soul of the dinner party, and the green light for further exposition.

So he began, "Not that Eliot, Mrs Latham, but the poet. He confounded the thesis of his great church predecessor John Donne."

Even Prunella, who had never been interested in religion but realized people who attended church were a minority, was baffled that what the vicar described as the 'two intellectual giants of the church' were daggers drawn at each other. She couldn't follow the remainder of what he said, neither could anyone else, but her view that books were silly was confirmed. She viewed the disagreement as nonsensical as if the two Co-op supermarkets in town entered into price rivalry with each other. Subsequent social chatter in the community revealed the conversation as the vicar's set piece, and Edna, the wife of the partner who attended an independent evangelical church, after much investigation said it all boiled down to the vicar wanting an expert in his congregation so that the church tower could be repointed at little or no cost.

Having left the library she thought, how odd to think of visiting the small aviary which formed part of the town zoo. The movement of the swallows to and from their nest viewed through a window that was made of one foot squares subdivided in this fashion by narrow strips of lead, seemed to offer some way out of a world which had disappeared with a finality like Pompeii completely covered by the lava which had erupted from Vesuvius. She recognized that it would be more sensible to go into town and look at and mingle with people, rather than find the zoo and search through it for the birds. She knew it existed because her husband was a trustee and it had retained its Edwardian title of Civic Zoological Gardens, Aviary and Arboretum. However it was now half past eleven in the morning, and she always waited until the second post at half past twelve, should there be any business letters for her husband, otherwise she would have driven into town immediately in her mini. She had almost arrived at the stage when she was beginning to feel like a criminal, not because of guilt but as she lacked any sort of alibi. The decision to wait for the post gave her complete reassurance because of what she had done, which was to reject her life as it had been just before she had started hoeing under the rhododendron bushes, and yet she could carry on as normal and no one would know what she would do. About that at this particular point she had no idea. The children would forget that the tea had not been ready, and they would attach no significance to her hoeing as they were accustomed occasionally to finding their mother engaged in a kind of one-off pursuit that did not recur. As it was a very hot summer there could be hundreds of reasons why their mother was hoeing beneath the bushes. At school projects which in the new fashionable learning had meant that algebra and the declension of Latin verbs jostled for attention with expeditions, water divining, or filling jam jars with water first above the town and then below the town to see the extent of urban pollution, and so domestic activity was soon dismissed as a project. In fact, home from an academic point of view was an adjunct of what occurred at school. The enormity, and insatiable erosion of their home life into the milieu of the school was illustrated by the fact that their mother, after one holiday, had refused to go abroad to a warm climate again. They were bemused in the geography lesson to learn that the tiny place on the south French coast, where they had their holiday, was only a fragment of world-wide locations which enjoyed a Mediterranean climate of hot dry summers, and warm wet winters. They did not think about their mother's detestation of very hot weather for long, but about the millions of people who lived in and enjoyed these conditions. Their mother therefore was a very singular person indeed of whom anything could be expected.

Prunella made her way towards the bushes to see if there had been revealed some overt sign of her state of mind.

Gazing down at the soil, her haphazard reckless activity with the hoe showed itself by small bits of undisturbed soil amid that which she had hopped about. Christopher would certainly not notice the tilled ground, and if he did would attach no significance to it. Since the financial papers had started to quote Australian shares he had to deal with customers who thought they would like to invest in this area which was outside that of his 'fixed assets and a good spread'. So he merely transmitted to his customers folios of printed advice obtained from a reputable firm in the City. In the same way she felt the garden was something about which he did not know enough to participate in discussion concerning it, and did not need to know when Prunella and the gardener planned everything with that meticulous attention of which he was reminded as far as his wife was concerned by the multicoloured quilt. Soon after the gardener had been hired Christopher had thought it courteous to have a chat with him about the weather and the old man had been so carried away with Prunella's enthusiasm that he assumed it was a joy shared by both husband and wife, and listened to a bit of Kipling the gardener remembered from his childhood at a village school; 'Some can pot begonias, and some can bud a rose . . . the glory of the garden it abideth not in words'. Such ecstasy Christopher found comforting in that he felt no responsibility for it was not his concern. He felt about it in much the same way as the ground coffee shop in town, from which an aroma permeated the air in its vicinity, because of the great effort made to obtain every variety of coffee; in a word others according to their various abilities were adding to the quality and content of matters, and such competence, whether it concerned Prunella, the gardener, or the owner of the coffee shop, only deserved praise, something he did not overtly indulge in because as a stockbroker dealing with customers, who sometimes thought they could become millionaires overnight, he was infinitely cautious.

Satisfied by the ground beneath the bushes the slack in Prunella's mind was taken up by watching two butterflies mating, and then disturbed by the spectacle of both being eaten by a house sparrow. But then a clean break was made with the garden and its predator, as she heard the familiar crunch of Mrs Hardcastle's cycle on the gravel drive delivering the second post. Mrs Hardcastle had taken the job with the post office during the war for a week or so until some male exempt from conscription could be found. It turned out that no one could be found, although in view of Mrs Hardcastle's efficiency and the necessity of women to help in the grave national emergency, the postmaster felt no obligation to search very hard. However, the war had been ended more than thirty years ago and at the age of nearly seventy Mrs Hardcastle was still delivering the post. Prunella had asked her casually one day when she arrived with a puncture in her bike tyre, soon patched by the gardener, if she had not thought about retiring. She had made this inquiry while Mrs Hardcastle was waiting for the bike, since Prunella had heard that old age pensions were being increased yet again. As she was essentially non-political the criticism that there was inflation too, could not be levelled against her because if necessary she would have listened to the students of the London School of Economics, and then the secretaries of Transport and General Workers Union, and the Amalgamated Union of Engineering Workers, all individually because she knew the sensitive nature of politics; but they would have judged her as completely reactionary for her view that if the mountains of beef and butter, there as a result of the common market, were made available this would be better than increasing pensions.

Mrs Hardcastle explained that her reason for not retiring was that in addition to delivering letters, she was a link between people and the social services, the women's auxiliary, meals on wheels, doctors, and chiropodists. With such a galaxy of people engaged in social work of one sort or another, Prunella had long decided that her efforts in this direction were superfluous and unrequired. Having taken the letters, she was not thinking of filling the vacuum in her life by voluntary work, but reverted to the cruel spectacle of two red admiral butterflies being eaten by a house sparrow while mating.

"I must do something," she said again but with a realization that some extraordinary effort would be required, and the last time she had made an extraordinary effort was when at the age of seventeen she grabbed Christopher's hand and plunged it inside the front of her dress in the lay-by. She was now thirty.

CHAPTER TWO

Within half an hour Prunella was in town eating part of her lunch of gammon, brussel sprouts and boiled potatoes, and the other portion of lemon meringue pie would be eaten in due course. She was sitting in Woolworths. A startling piece of information causing great confusion among those who do not know that Woolworths' cafeterias serve very good food. A visiting merchant banker who stayed at The Oaks, a name the Lathams had retained for their home when they bought it, one weekend, when told to lunch there by Prunella considered the obvious riposte was to say, absolutely solemnly and without any thought of being facetious, "Did you enjoy working there and in what department were you employed?"

As usual she was at no loss for an answer and said that it should be in Ronay's good food guide with one star more than anywhere else. A reply which the merchant banker then thought absolutely charming but never for one moment, being a habitué of his club and The Ritz where he took what he called his bites in the great metropolis, did he think Prunella actually ate food in Woolworths. Of course, these circumstances are not surprising to the British, who have observed the incredible effort made by their fellow countrymen who know how to spot a loan stock which will rise rapidly, to make themselves at home in Chinese restaurants by asking with the greatest fuss possible where the lavatory is, but just in case they have made a faux pas ensure the four walls of the place resound with the information that they are bound for winter skiing and are taking a different route on this occasion. To those who actually decide on the quality of the food they eat in Chinese restaurants, the opinion is almost always favourable. Prunella realized that her choice of restaurant was incredulous to the merchant banker, and it was a sense of clash of severance which had decided her to go into town, rather than brood further about what she should do, particularly as the half-formed idea to find the town aviary, after a little introspection, seemed absurd. The postwoman had delivered no mail that she could have taken to her husband's office.

To the foreigner British society appears very fluid. There are never any revolutions. Academics, businessmen, and politicians from abroad know that there is a presence, as it were, of the upper class. A curator of a foreign museum bringing some treasures to be auctioned in London will no doubt be invited for the weekend to some mansion, whose owner's name appears with others on the notepaper of the auctioneering firm, and see priceless objects of every description hanging on walls, reposing on library shelves, placed in glass-fronted cabinets, standing in every alcove, and gracing as a centrepiece a spacious dining room. It is a presence, an elusive presence, disappearing and reappearing, a chameleon but occasionally revealed in flagrante delicto as powerful socially and politically today as it was a hundred years ago. Its strength is maintained by the simple expedient of adding to its ranks carefully selected life peers. When Prunella finally decides what it is she has to do it is vital to realize that she is a beautiful woman endowed with perfect dinner-party manners and quite exquisite conversation, sometimes ambiguous but if so always capable of an inoffensive interpretation.

It is no exaggeration to say that had she been so minded she could have been a diplomat's wife, or something similar at the fulcrum of power in London; she was endowed as described but was without that nervous hesitation, which in some derives from reading books, and leads to inertia. Had she been so minded all sorts of opportunities could have been taken because of the people she met by being the wife of her husband. When the old family loyalty to the Liberal Party was replaced by becoming Conservative, because the local Liberals would not support a direct grant school opting out of the state system when comprehensive schools were made compulsory, the local Conservative MP had let it be known that he would like to be invited to a weekly dinner party. He was divorced, but Prunella at this time, in fact all the time from when she had plunged Christopher's hand down the front of her dress until yesterday afternoon, had never for one moment considered infidelity of any kind. Even her thoughts were pure as the driven snow. No man faced with such formidable array of beauty combined with her conversation, which was self-effacing and yet so shrewd, would have dared to take a sexual initiative of any kind.

In the present period of inflation, Christopher and the other partners invited all sorts of people to dinner thinking her charm would in some indefinable way dissuade them from buying antiques of every kind which they thought would not depreciate and about which the partners knew nothing, and persuade them that 'fixed assets and a good spread' was still the best policy. The partners knew their business, and in her usual casual fashion Prunella would throw in some sort of remark which placed the retention of shares as beyond question. A large insurance firm had its head office in the town, and Prunella had convinced the chairman, quite out of mind because he could not in his annual state that several old masters had been acquired together with two Meissen dinner services, to invest in stocks and shares because if he bought paintings and pottery, which anyway he could not do, the firm would be turned into a museum. Later she said when the market recovered he could obtain something for the boardroom, a memento of the crisis, which would inconspicuously but very effectively prove to his fellow directors that he was aware of what was happening, and had at all times been master of the situation.

The panic had now disappeared, but while it lasted Prunella found herself dining with all sorts of people from at home and abroad. It became known, because most people decided to retain their shares after being a guest at one of the dinner parties, that distraught financial advisors of every sort endeavoured to obtain a dinner invitation for their clients. The firm was very old, as old as the town which was a product of the industrial revolution, and in the panic people seemed to want to investigate every asset they had; to look at it fondly lest by next day it would be worthless. Many people, after calm had returned, sent invitations for their dinner parties, and it would have been no trouble at all for Prunella to have been swept in to that London orientated pond where the panic had no doubt originated, and whose swimmers thought they controlled the destiny of the world. The panic had convinced her that this countrywide and even, to a less extent, worldwide panic which had swept back and forth over their dinner parties, represented a fettered world.

She said to herself, "They've got no common sense," but only to herself for she saw they were at the centre of a maelstrom where an indiscreet word might cause a great deal of damage.

By the time it had passed she had a shrewd idea of not only national financial and political affairs but those of places abroad also. The sound advice people received led others to suppose that in some way they possessed influence, and matters of national consequence were confided to the six regular diners. Did they know, said the merchant banker, that the man with most power in the country was an Oxford don? Did they know, said a duke, the only peer as a matter of fact who they met during the crisis, and who came to see how much his shares were worth in a canal company which had only acquired 100 yards of land before people switched to railways, that the man with most power in the country was a member of the House of Lords? Did they know, said the vicar's wife – who as the daughter of a man who had made a fortune in some way or other and felt she could ignore finance because of its simplicity, but became so excited by the swirl of events and felt called upon to reveal the distilled wisdom of university gossip in which she recently participated – that Widmerpool did not exist?

"Who?" Christopher thinking some financial scandal was about to shake the City.

The vicar explained that his wife was merely talking about a series of novels considered to portray the British establishment, and that he and his wife completely disassociated themselves from the remark which had been made at high table by a foreign academic.

The town had a population of 250,000 so although Prunella might meet someone she recognized in the cafeteria, it frequently happened that she went in and out without seeing anyone she knew. She had been educated locally at a girl's direct grant school so this increased the possibility of meeting an acquaintance, and in fact most of her afternoons in town were spent in haphazard casual conversation sooner or later before she returned home to get tea ready for the children. She had chosen an empty table as she could not see a familiar face, and her mind relapsed once more to the circumstances of her marriage with Christopher, and the spectacle of the bird devouring the butterflies. She suddenly realized that what she desired was not being like a partner in her husband's firm but actually to control a man. Whether she wished to mutilate him is a matter at this point of idle conjecture, but such an event was a possibility in view of the manner in which she arrived at her decision. She knew from gossip and her own experience how vulnerable some men are to pleasures of the flesh. The fact of the matter was that when she had plunged Christopher's hand down the front of her dress despite his drunken stupor the fine quality of her lingerie, its silkiness, seemed to activate some mechanism in his hands. She was astonished because she thought he was too drunk to go further, and would just have a strong enough impression in his mind of what she might look like naked from a stage just beyond necking but only just as to ensure marriage. She knew however that she had the situation under control and he did indeed go further than she intended, delighted by the natural vigour of his animal behaviour. He did not, though, get below her waist. At this point she stopped him, although fascinated at the way he undid a button, and unclipped her bra strap. She wasn't a cold woman, but neither did she intend to be an easy lay, so she told him to wait until they were married. At which point he appeared to become comatose. It was not until she arrived home that she realized that in the confusion following his collapse back into a drunken stupor, when she had to do up her dress and decide to drive the car herself, she had forgotten to put her bra back on.

The next morning when Christopher found the bra on the floor of the car he wanted to mention it to Prunella so as to make his proposal of marriage informal, but as the incident had occurred quite unexpectedly didn't want to emphasize in any way what he considered she might think as having taken advantage of her dress having only one single button at the back. He therefore told her that the prize she had given to be raffled at the next meeting of the Young Farmer's Club had resulted in a record sale of tickets. Both understood what he meant and the matter was never referred to again.

She was just finishing her meringue pie when she said to herself, "I will never make that mistake again," having arrived at the firm conclusion that she would allow no other man than her husband to take her bra off, and also that unpleasant consequences might ensue from leaving bras in the house of another man's wife. It would just be an adventure, for it never occurred to her that she might divorce her husband, and at the same time assumed the man she would ensnare would be about her own age and married.

Prunella was just about to go, now certain of what she must do, when she recognized the voice of Cynthia Stapleton saying, "Hello." They had been in the same class at the girls' grammar school, and as in addition to eating in Woolworths they both bought most of their children's clothes in the store, they always had much about which they could talk. The fact that Christopher Latham and his partners were worth between them in the region of two to three million pounds was not only unknown to Cynthia when she asked Prunella's advice about a 5p per week insurance policy, but was also for that matter unknown to Prunella, although she realized that their house, lifestyle, their preference of Scarborough to Sardinia for holidays did not reflect the money her husband and his colleagues had. Although they could each have bought an island in the Hebrides or the Aegean Sea, they did not because the tradition of the firm for the past one hundred years had been to regard all money as being at the disposal of the firm in the general interests of the town, and indeed of the country. They did not only buy stocks and shares for other people but carried on every conceivable financial transaction and advice, but all was done with the greatest discretion, and its success depended on the careful selection of personnel; in their own office they had two clerks who had graduated from university in accountancy and company law. It was impossible for every interest to be remembered, but all business activity in the town was indexed so any connection, no matter how distant it lay in the past, could be looked up, and in a separate index was to be found all their contacts, investments, and indeed people they indirectly employed. If necessary they were ruthless but kind; the London stockbrokers through whom they did their business in the City were never reminded of the fact that they were financially in the pocket of Latham, Blakeshaw and Smithers, and would not be provided they continued to operate efficiently.

When Cynthia Stapleton had mentioned that she wished to take out a 5p per week insurance policy, Prunella made a note of her name and said her husband would send someone round in the morning, and by 9.30 of that morning a name was found in the index, and an hour later the first 5p had been collected, and a form left for Cynthia's husband to forward to the tax office for the rebate allowed on insurance policies. Prunella had never asked herself why only 5p had been invested, and the truth was that Cynthia's husband was against the capitalist system and regarded the 5p as equated in some fashion with Oliver Twist asking for a second helping in the workhouse.

Of course he was perfectly entitled to his point of view, and one is at pains to be impartial for there is no intention here to introduce a subjective political tract, the Chairman of the Chinese Communist Party, Paul Foot, and speaker after speaker at Labour Party Conferences are against the capitalist system. Latham, Blakeshaw and Smithers had been selling unit trusts to people in all of life since the 1930s, although they preferred to invest people's money directly in shares, (and had been obtaining these also for people in all walks of life since the 1930s) because they felt their investment advice was better than that in London.

Cynthia was saying considering the very hot summer her husband had decided to grow some grapes, knowing that Prunella was interested in gardening for she always purchased her seeds personally. Prunella for her part was wondering if Cynthia's husband would be a suitable victim for her plan of seduction decided on about fifteen minutes earlier, and then ruled him out because he did not attend the dinner parties.

The dinner parties had become the centre piece of the Lathams' social life. They had originated in the necessity to consume a vast quantity of wine that the partners had fortuitously acquired. The wine came into their possession as a result of a by-election in 1935 when the Liberals lost the seat, which they had held as long as anyone could remember and was associated with the business activity of the town, to the Conservatives in the most peculiar circumstances. The chairman of the local Liberal Party went out of his mind, but this factor was not generally known and the electorate assumed that his actions were those of a sane man carried out in the malevolent deliberation. It was not until his firm went into liquidation that what occurred was revealed in the bankruptcy hearings which preceded the by-election by one year, so there was adequate time for everyone to hear the full story, or what they had at first thought was the full story until further bizarre details became more widely known. Details so bizarre that no one doubted their authenticity. They involved bankruptcy and the loss of four hundred jobs in the hosiery trade. The chairman of the local Liberal Party was the only shareholder in the company for whose failure he was responsible. He simply withdrew large sums of money from the firm believing after a sudden decline of orders that the capitalist system was about to collapse. His motive was to use the money for some purpose to ingratiate himself with the new masters of the Bolshevik millennium, which was just round the corner. He remembered from his schooldays the financial disaster known as the South Sea Bubble, when speculators lost heavily. To get to the South Seas one had to travel across water which was free. He thought by investing in wine which was liquid like water, but unlike it cost a great deal of money, was being shrewd and was indicating the severity of the approaching crisis. As room after room of his house became filled with cases of wine he convinced his close relatives that they should say nothing about it in the interests of good business. He had the water in his fountain in the garden impregnated with a red dye, explaining that he was experimenting with a new range of chemical additives for hosiery garments, and the problem was to simulate conditions in a mangle, as washing machines were then unknown. Everyone accepted the explanation, even people associated with the technical aspects of the industry, because in an age of scientific progress it was accepted that the innovator was aware of factors unknown to them. Latham, Blakeshaw and Smithers were entrusted with sorting out the mess in the most discreet manner. That is how they acquired their wine. They filled the remaining rooms which had none, and continued to replenish the stock to the present day.

If Prunella had been a different person, in a different place at a different time she would have behaved differently after she had said goodbye to Cynthia. If she had been Cleopatra she would have been putting an aphrodisiac in the welcome drink prepared for the Roman, Mark Antony. No doubt Lady Godiva had a particular man in mind when she rode stark naked on a horse through the streets of Coventry. At half past two on this August afternoon in Andchestford Prunella, had she wanted to, and had she known the venues where such encounters happened, could without doubt have picked up a member of the opposite sex. Her mood was of this wide kind, but her immediate inclination was to confirm her existing assets, and so she made her way towards her husband's office to have a look at him. She was not in the habit of going there without purpose and as she had no post to deliver had quickly to think of a reason for her visit. So when she arrived at the office she asked her husband whether he wanted any wine fetched for the dinner party that evening. She always showed him the menu on a Monday when it was their turn for the dinner party and he always selected the wines, about which she knew nothing, and ensured they were there for the Wednesday dinner. Some wine was kept in the house cellar, but the bulk of it was in the house that had belonged to the mad chairman of the local Liberal Party. In the past she had sometimes called in the office to see if any wine was required, but normally her husband would collect any required on the way home from work. She had no ulterior motive for closing her mind to what was what as regards wines, but regarded the process of selection as quite ridiculous when she found that she simply disliked some wines and liked others and that eating fish or roast beef did not induce a taste for the wine that convention required should accompany that particular dish. The whole subject was once and for all settled in her mind when a review by her husband's firm of continental shares led to an Austrian stockbroker being at dinner. In casual conversation with Christopher about business at the office the Austrian had revealed that he had a vineyard, and naturally Christopher insisted that wine from his region should be taken with the meal. Indeed Prunella was far from being a slave to any convention if she was so inclined. Austrian rosé therefore led Prunella to comment that the wine tasted different, and that she liked it. Whereupon with a great deal of historical detail their guest explained that particular wines with specified dishes was a successful conspiracy by the French aristocracy, and that Portuguese rosé and German Mosel had only been included as acceptable as a means of camouflage. It came as no surprise to Prunella that the French aristocracy was capable of such duplicity, as she had already written off the British aristocracy after visiting the fashionable London shops and seeing the rubbish they purchased there. She was quite certain of the superiority of Woolworths and their Winfield range of products.

Her husband seemed his normal self, which in view of her somewhat excited state of mind she found reassuring, and calmly in his usual manner handed her a slip of paper on which was written 'two bottles of Château Mouton Rothschild 1964'. The house was in a suburb, and she merely had to drive there which was about ten minutes, collecting the key from the caretaker in the small lodge cottage. She was quite convinced by this time that she was about to embark on some sexual escapade as pictures of eligible men with whom she had dined flitted in and out of her mind. She soon collected the two bottles as all the wine was arranged alphabetically and then by year. Wiping the dust off the bottles she noticed the wine was red, and vague thoughts of virile and vulnerable past male dinner guests crystallized in her mind into a bunch of cherries. From there she was able to deduce from what had hitherto been pushed into an obscure corner of her mind, that this evening's guest was an actor from the local theatre, of which one of the partners was a trustee, and that it all had something to do with fruit, and in particular cherries. She knew as the play was still running, that she would see it on the billboards on the way home. There it was, *The Cherry Orchard* by Anton Chekhov, and as she drove home she remembered a few words Christopher had said about it when he told her that their guest was acting in the current production at the Argosy, as the refurbished music hall was known. To those who visit Andchestford the fact that it was a Victorian building was in no way to its discredit; it was small and had those curved boxes which reach out to the stage together to ensure that the architect at least has done his task of indicating the possible importance of what was happening on the stage. She remembered that he had said that it was about an old family who had refused to make a sensible business decision and sell part of the estate, a cherry orchard, so that the rest could be retained. By the time she had arrived home Prunella had decided she could not convey her feeling about the play by an arrangement of rhododendron leaves in the middle of the dining table; the rhododendron bushes being the nearest relative to a tree they had in the garden. What she required was several small branches from a variety of trees to indicate that it was necessary to sell the cherry trees; the foliage of many trees in the centre of the table would show that had the right decision been made nothing essential would have been sacrificed.

She decided to ring the Arboretum. Those in Andchestford who did not know what the Arboretum was soon made it their business to find out because of its unusual name. She explained who she was, the wife of a trustee for the partners were entrusted with a great deal in the town, and inquired which was the nearest way to it in view of the new one-way streets, not wishing to reveal her ignorance of its location. She then told him that she required twigs with foliage from six commonly found British trees, and that if it was not inconvenient she would collect them that afternoon. She obtained what she wanted, and arrived home again at half past five. The children had been at home for an hour, but were no way perturbed by their mother's absence. It would be difficult to think of anything in respect of their mother or anyone else which would perturb them, for they were children of the world.

Prunella was now like a general in the RASC examining his logistics for the landing operation in Normandy in the war, although having been born in 1946 a comparison with a military operation did not occur to her. As with the nineteen-twenties furniture which had been an expression of mood until she had started hoeing under the rhododendron bushes, she now quickly fastened on to a comparison with her present position. Her husband and his partners had with great ingenuity prevented the principal hotel in the town The Darlington, which was completely independent, from being taken over by a national chain. She remembered the excitement, the sense of betrayal when her husband confided to her when the other partners, their wives, and two guests had departed, that that very day the alderman, who with his wife had been the guests, and who held 20% of the shares, had sold out. Had sold out indeed even before the take-over price which he expected to be raised several times yet was still at its initial stage when the chain were merely testing the ground.

"A stupid man," her husband confided to her.

The comparison appealed to her because stupidity was prosaic and despite the great drama of which it was part, placed the matter in the real world, where it was essential in order to attain one's objective to be clever. Her husband continued that the alderman's family, which had always voted Conservative, had lost its nerve after the Liberal landslide of 1906, and had only seemed to recover it in 1951 after the Conservative victory in the general election of that year, which had led to the guest who was the present object of ridicule successfully contesting a seat on the local council.

Prunella's attitude to business as a whole, as distinct from her marriage to Christopher which was really the result of him being a wealthy man, was naive in the extreme until her interest was aroused when she would become as acute in her analysis of the situation as any asset stripper, and it was the aura of asset stripping which was disturbing the serene atmosphere of Andchestford's business life of which Latham, Blakeshaw and Smithers was the centre. Prunella's analytic ability when intrigued would only extend to assimilating the pertinent facts, and then as the financial world her attention would disappear and her attitude resume its normal indolence as regards such matters. Shortly after marriage her husband had bought her £100 of shares which he said she should follow and see how well they did. He had said so at breakfast but by the time he returned home from work the same day she had forgotten all about them. He did not of course forget, but an incident as certain in its finality as her later rejection of the Mediterranean climate had occurred which led Christopher to realize that there was a category of subjects in which not he but his wife would always take the initiative. She had refused also soon after marriage to invite her best school friend to a dinner party. It had nothing to do with Jennifer being the daughter of a labourer at a brick quarry, of this Christopher was quite certain, because when asked who she would like invited to the wedding Prunella had written Jennifer's name at the top of the list, and she had already been to one dinner party. As Prunella had the easiest social relations with all her acquaintances, and Christopher was aware of the value of such a wife, he surmised that somewhere there was sufficient reason for her abstruse behaviour. What he did not know, and what Jennifer had confided to Prunella, was that she had seduced a curate and intended to get a divorce after the marriage as soon as possible. Such conduct Prunella resolved to give as wide a berth as possible. Jennifer had a waspish figure, at most times a demure pretty face but whose expression could change rapidly from solemn and plain to coquettish and enticing beauty. She also had very good legs, which part of her repertory Prunella had no doubt been used to seduce the curate. She and Prunella had been friends because of their common interest in jewellery. Jennifer was known to Prunella to take lightly those physical attributes with which she had so remarkably been endowed, and it was Prunella's knowledge of what really made Jennifer tick that caused the end of their friendship and this was her reputation as a thinker.

Christopher, after finishing his remarks at the general election of 1951, felt compelled to continue about the alderman and his family, and to add his reflections upon the national economy, when Prunella said to her husband "Surely, Chris, the takeover of the The Darlington will do no harm. You, Don and Mr Hetherington, the three partners, have assets all over the place."

"Too jejune, my dear," replied Christopher.

Prunella had no idea of what her husband meant by jejune, but she was used to the odd word she did not understand late at night when Christopher was well and truly away from his business colleagues, the majority of whom would not have understood either, as they did not do crosswords with the intensity with which Christopher did them, and on which, by one of the clerks in the office who had a similar interest, he was acknowledged as an expert.

He then added, "And antediluvian."

Prunella knew that his natural courtesy would lead him to make himself quite clear, and she thought beyond 'peradventure'. She had, when her husband started using these unusual words late at night, begun to look up a few in the dictionary, and peradventure being the first, she remembered its meaning. She thought they were all in some way connected with stocks and shares, hearing other words like 'monetary' and 'fiduciary', which fell into the same bracket in her mind, spoken at the dinner parties.

"His father," continued Christopher, "sold him stock in the railways in 1924."

"The railways?" inquired Prunella.

"Yes the railways," he explained, "and did so because the first Labour government of 1924, despite it being a minority one, he thought was about to confiscate all property. As regards the firm, and their takeover people, there's no comparison. They are merely taking advantage of temporary difficulties, a fall in trade, which happens from time to time. Far better to leave things as they are, and not close them down, and they will still be there when trade looks up. We should know, Pru, because the firm has been involved in business for over a century."

In the event Prunella witnessed at dinner parties a type of conversation that had never characterized them before, and had never done so again. Her husband, Mr Hetherington, the senior partner only by age, and Donald Jones who was of Christopher's generation, giving what amounted to lectures about the nature of the business world. These sufficed to win the day, and the firm's liquid assets of between two to three million pounds were not required to thwart the asset strippers.

It was with such a comparison in mind that Prunella approached the dinner party that evening. In the euphoria following the repulse of the attempts to take over the Argosy, the management had placed the catering staff and waiters at the disposal of the partners for their weekly dinner parties. Some felt that the spirit of Dunkirk had prevailed. Those to whom the war was history successfully had the senior party, Mr Hetherington, made an honorary lecturer at the town's college of education.

The hotel was always paid for the services of the cook and waiter who came to one of the houses each week, and always seemed to be able to provide by Wednesday the menus prepared on the previous Monday by Prunella, Sarah Hetherington or Edna Jones. If Prunella was in her plans intent on repeating the skill which had resulted in the defeat of the asset strippers, she could do nothing before half past eight when the dinner was due to start except to ask the waiter to put the small branches from the Arboretum in a punchbowl used as a flower vase. It was Victorian and bought for her by Christopher soon after marriage as a birthday present when he saw that his wife was collecting furniture and bric-a-brac. He had subsequently noticed the difference in design between the bowl and what Prunella herself purchased, and had thought it as well not to venture into this field again, and he had asked her subsequently what she wanted. When she had replied that being married to him was like having a birthday present every day he had been at a loss for what to say, but decided that although Prunella had seemed completely serious the incident was unfinished. He compared it with the bra left in the car, and decided that dexterity would surmount the difficulty, for after all the incident of the bra had been potentially more dangerous. Prunella was pregnant at the time so he told her that he thought giving presents was a convention the child would expect, and she agreed to accept a box of chocolates twice a year, on her birthday and at Christmas. Christopher had spent some time phrasing his reply because he wished to make it inclusive of all occasions, and delayed it until he was satisfied that no possible anniversary, where a present was vital, was omitted. He pondered, and rejected the idea of a gift on their wedding anniversary. His evaluation of the situation, which he thought was one of great delicacy, was to do simply as she asked, and give her the chocolates twice a year.

By eight thirty all were eating their soup, and the predatory female was wondering why Don, the partner about her own age who was certainly not as good looking as the film star in the last picture she had seen, but she noted was in no way disfigured, had married Edna; and she thought about the marriage between the two all through the meal.

The actor when he arrived, because of his age, had immediately reminded Prunella of her father. Not in any way interested in the actor, Chekhov, or the arrangement of leaves, Prunella did not make any comment when the conversation began with desultory remarks about the very hot weather. Prunella had not abandoned her strategy of some sort of sexual adventure, but on seeing the actor the whole scheme was temporarily shelved. She was too apathetic to mention the small branches which stood in the punchbowl in the centre of the table, having decided no damaging inference of any kind could be drawn from them, and that they fell in the category of the spoons with which they were eating their soup, and the colour of the ceiling which could not be seen in the subdued light. They did not usually have any centrepiece for the dining table at the weekly gatherings and Prunella, before any of the guests arrived, and knowing that her husband thought her perfect, had nevertheless in view of the grand strategy in her mind which she resolved would take care of any eventuality real or imagined, decided to tell him that his remarks about the play had given her a wonderful idea; the object of the centrepiece was therefore explained to Christopher, whose reaction was to thank the fates who had enabled him to make this remarkable woman his wife. When nothing was said about the centrepiece by Prunella while they were eating their soup, Christopher, knowing that there had never been one before at a dinner party, and that it was Prunella's idea, introduced it into the conversation with greatest circumspection. It then came to him why his wife had said nothing. She wished to be fair; he had originated the conception by pointing out that the owners of the estate in *The Cherry Orchard* had no business sense; and consequently Prunella did not wish to take credit from what he had originated. In view of the fact that it was the middle of August and that game was somewhere on the menu, the shooting season he knew began on the twelfth of August, he wondered whether the combination of leaves from the Arboretum and the overt criticism they implied of the owners of a country estate, and the eating of grouse, would lead to gossip in London where the actor normally worked. He knew that owners of country estates had much influence in the City. His thoughts were travelling very rapidly just as if his eyes were absorbing the figures that were significant in a company report. To mention the leaves, he concluded, would only be a pleasant gesture soon forgotten, as he remembered that he, Christopher Latham, did in fact own a grouse moor, and that today everybody ate grouse. "The rich man in his castle, the poor man at his gate, God made them high or lowly, and ordered their estate". The hymn remembered from the school assembly was ringing in his ears, and he thought of contemporary society in which all could eat grouse, as contrasted with the old days when it was restricted to a few. He felt completely right about his intention to say something about the leaves. (In parenthesis it should be noted at point that the singing of the hymn in school assembly, which Christopher remembered being sung quite often, did not indicate the existence of reactionaries of the worst kind at work in Andchestford, it was merely that the headmaster somehow got confused over the numbers of the various hymns in the assembly book. It happened about every three months and it always resulted in the same hymn being played. Various theories were put forward to explain the headmaster's conduct: he was a progressive Conservative, a Marxist Socialist, an agnostic or an atheist.)

"The leaves are there just for your benefit, Mr Ranville," said Christopher.

Mr Hetherington, who was not in his dotage, about sixty, and whose intellect as far as business was concerned seemed to improve with age, added, "And you can tell your friends in London that we have Dutch elm disease well under control here in Andchestford."

"That's not the idea at all, Hether," said Prunella. She always called him Hether, and the only conceivable situation when she would think such a form of address inappropriate would be if she were the toastmaster at a banquet at which he was one of the principal guests. It expressed the consensus in the firm that his daughter, who was an unknown quantity except for the fact that she was an artist, a peripatetic artist communicating only with her mother and father at Christmas from such diverse places as London, Manchester and Paris, would in due course be found an appropriate position in the firm.

She continued, "I thought it would be nice to show what most people would have done with the estate in the play. Just sell part of it, and all sorts of trees could have been planted in the hedgerows."

"I am sure," said Mr Ranville, "that Mr Latham finds your advice invaluable, and the City could well do with some of it."

Donald Jones usually kept his conversation to banal pleasantries to such an extent indeed that when he did realize an effort was required, despite its incisive nature, most people thought he was just talking in his usual fashion. Unlike Prunella he did not think books silly, but he was the one person who did regard her as silly because she seemed empty-headed and superficial. It was not her comments about the play which he thought typified her limitless ignorance, which he found no difficulty in tolerating and which he regarded as so profound as to manifest itself on every occasion they met, which led him to make one of his rare closely argued interventions, it was the knowledge that Mr Ranville might in some way convey an impression of ineptitude on the part of Andchestford's financial community to London, still smarting over the failure to take over The Darlington. It was clearly out of the question to give intimate details of financial transactions to impress their visitor, so he thought he would talk about the play which he had seen to divert attention from finance, and also convince their guest that Andchestford was not an intellectual bog.

"I've had difficulty getting tickets for today's matinee," said Donald. "Was it a satisfying performance?" The Argosy always had a matinee Wednesday afternoon, and no performance in the evening.

"It has been for the whole three weeks' run from the first night," replied Mr Ranville. "What had seemed a casual acquaintance was converted into solid friendship after someone was heard sobbing in the audience when at the end of the play the family take their leave of the old house while the cherry orchard is still intact."

"Sentimental nonsense," said Donald, who during his long apprenticeship before he took over from his uncle in the firm had read widely but deeply in the most eclectic manner. It had been regarded as more sensible not to send him to university but allow him an articled clerk to master the vast complexity of the firm; which he did during the day and ravaged the local library on the way home from work to fill his adolescent evenings, which he continued to fill in exactly the same way after he married Edna, who was plain and very serious, and whose only reading other than the authorized version of the Bible was a concordance of the scriptures in which she looked up references after the midweek Bible study group at the town's principal independent evangelical chapel, attendance which constituted their only mutual activity before marriage. In view of the necessity of attending the Wednesday dinner parties, and because the Bible study group also met on a Wednesday evening, a change of minister at the chapel had been taken as an ideal opportunity without fuss or bother to move the study group to Thursday, as Donald, both as an elder and by virtue of his skill in exposition, was without doubt of great importance at the Bible meeting. There arose no question of priorities between the two events because the felicitous arrival of a new minister whose enthusiasm was shown by the transfer of the group to the next evening in the week, together with other profound but impeccably orthodox changes in the activities of the chapel, ensured that no inference could be made as regards the dinner party. For those who like to dilate about events which in fact will never take place, had a choice been inevitable Donald and Edna would have attended the Bible study group. Donald was a sincere person, and no one doubted his integrity, not only of deeds but thoughts. It is advisable to make his position clear before Prunella's opinion of him, which is undoubtedly correct, is stated. He was closely identified with the chapel; his great grandfather had laid one of its foundation stones, and a continuing family loyalty to it had never varied with the years; and several other families, artisan and entrepreneur, shop steward and member of the ASTMS (Clive Jenkins' union), had shown the same loyalty and common purpose ever since the chapel was built. Edna was the daughter of a clerk whose entire working life had been spent calculating National Insurance contributions and sticking the several hundred stamps each week on benefit cards. Prunella considered Donald's association with the chapel as completely fortuitous, and all due to his father. It is not the intention to deprecate members of independent chapels, and had Donald been a Methodist, Roman Catholic, Church of England or Jew her assessment would have been the same, and indubitably equally true. She told Christopher, after meeting the couple for a year, that had Donald's father been an atheist he would have been one as well, to which emphatic remark Christopher readily agreed, never thinking to add that this opinion should go no further. He knew his wife and she was torpid, languid and indolent. She was the only person who had observed him on the few occasions when his incisive manner was at work and when his conclusions seemed to her to be outside the sphere of his religious belief, from which after a year's acquaintance she had severed him in her mind. He was handsome in a statuesque manner, and the only time she thought about him was when she passed the Crimea Memorial in the Town Hall Square and noticed the clothed armed warriors with shields and swords and heads adorned with circlets of laurel.

Donald expanded his opening salvo describing the play, "Sentimental nonsense if taken literally, but Chekhov didn't intend that it should be taken literally. He wanted to convey a social message. I don't say I have the same intimate knowledge of Russia in the second half of the nineteenth century as Chekhov, but enough to understand what the play is really about. First you must be quite clear that Chekhov was integrated into the society about which he wrote, for he was a country doctor. If you belonged to the upper classes, and everyone who could establish such a connection did, no matter how tenuous the link you could rely on help, financial help to ensure that position in society to which you had been born, in the event of it being in danger. Some prince perhaps, ruling vast provinces of Asiatic Russia, could be called upon by a landed family, perhaps without title, but providing an officer cadet for the Tsar's army. The prince would restore a family like that in *The Cherry Orchard* to that life to which they had been accustomed for generations.

"Chekhov knew it, his audience knew it, the whole of Russia knew it. The family at the end of the play is not being turned out into the streets; the aristocratic fund was limitless. What does happen is that Chekhov induces in his audience's state of mind a question, a political social question."

"And what was that question?" asked Prunella, who by now had placed Donald in that vacuum created by the actor reminding her of her father.

Just like her to make an obvious and irrelevant remark, thought Donald, and then continued, "I am glad you asked me that because it was not a question as we normally understand it, but a social conundrum. Where, Chekhov wanted his audience to ask, should the family be going – instead of to an exact replica of the estate they were now leaving provided by the limitless aristocratic fund? I believe I have the answer. But amongst the people, the serfs to whom the Tsar had recently given complete freedom."

Lest the actor should think Donald's remarks were a set piece carefully rehearsed by a provincial bookworm, he thought it best to leave their guest, who generally resided in London, with a picture of wide culture and voluble brilliance.

He knew, from his few excursions into the dinner parties of the country's metropolis from where the participants thought they ruled the world, that his efforts lay far ahead of that assortment of diners, where the recital of confidential information of one sort or another sufficed to the exclusion of nearly all else, that their guest would find it difficult, if he were impartial, to fault his dinner conversation. It will have become obvious by now that Donald was a mine of information, and within his ambit fell the thought processes of London's exclusive diners. He, as an inhabitant of Andchestford, was not privy to those confidential reports compiled by the permanent civil service, and shackled to ministers elected by the people for entirely different purposes; the insatiable lust for power, and ability to hack at the vitals of the country was well known, as confidential reports occasionally found their way into newspapers before they reached the minister; not by accident but intention, in what was thought of as a master *coup de grâce*, for in the furore other equally dangerous reports would be adopted by shackled ministers and not noticed in the confession caused by the odd leak of information.

Donald had therefore a handicap which he now proceeded to remedy, and accomplished it with his usual consummate skill. Christopher, Edna and Mr and Mrs Hetherington had little idea about the nature of his conversation, and as it occurred infrequently never gave it a further thought. Prunella did notice, had noticed, and come to the conclusion that Donald's position as an elder of the independent evangelical chapel was hereditary, and from her opinion of fashionable shops in London and the taste they displayed, she had a scathing opinion of the peerage. The net result of these shades of thought mingling in her head was to regard Donald as some sort of phantom, whom Edna could twist round her little finger. Quite unlike Christopher, who did not realize that his tentative behaviour towards his wife was reciprocated by Prunella who firmly appreciated that there were at least two things on which he would not budge. He would never conspire with anyone to defraud the firm, and he would divorce her without hesitation on receiving conclusive evidence that she had committed adultery.

In order to leave no misunderstanding in the mind of their guest as to the wide culture of Andchestford, Donald thought a disquisition about opera in the eighteenth century would be appropriate, and he now began, "A social purpose, although of a very different kind, motivated opera during most of the eighteenth century when the ferment from France caused by, for example, Voltaire and Rousseau, led to musical compositions which emphasized the existing political order. A French abbé, nominally an ecclesiastic, would write lyrics translated by an Italian for an opera composed by an Austrian and commissioned by a Bavarian.

"To look at the whole question from another angle, consider the proposition that in Wagner's opera from the Ring cycle 'The Ride of the Valkyries' is a singular charming piece in a pile of dross."

Prunella, her mood now centred on Donald, thought, 'I could give you a good ride,' and thinking some intervention in her strategy imperative moved like quicksilver to an occasion when Donald had said something about Beethoven; she therefore interrupted "Don, do tell us about Beethoven again."

"Very well," he said, thinking quite rightly that the visitor was now suitably impressed by the wide culture of Andchestford. "However you will think me very reactionary. The *Emperor Concerto* was composed not in praise of Napoleon but of Beethoven's real if not actual patron, the Austrian Emperor, who would soon by the arts of diplomacy contain the conquests of the French."

Mr Ranville, who knew that Vienna was in Austria – indeed it not being the intention to suggest that he was in any way an ignoramus, was full of information both serious and trifling, and could hold his own anywhere – said Beethoven was difficult but enjoyable, complex like Austrian confections of which the gateau he was now eating recalled. Mr Hetherington who never knew from quite where his artist daughter would send her next greeting, asked if he might make a note of the addresses where these masterpieces of confectionery could be eaten.

Prunella, in a sort of daze at her audacity with regard to Donald, who seemed across the table to be wearing a laurel on his head and stripped naked to the waist – she could not see any more of him due to the height of the table – wondered whether or not, but said nothing to her guests, she might start collecting these confections; a bewilderment of only a few seconds' duration when she quickly apprehended that one doesn't collect cakes, but eats them.

CHAPTER THREE

Next morning, after being awake for about fifteen minutes, Prunella kept visualizing the large tracts of moor which lay to the north of the town, and superimposed on what to her was a bleak landscape entirely bereft of any sign of activity, was the figure of Donald Jones. There was not even a sheep or the odd car on the tarmacked track at first, but Prunella had a keen sense of reality and before her husband and the children had left for work and school the sheep and the car had appeared. It was not the need to get the breakfast that made the moors persistent and total in their monopoly of her thoughts, but a previous experience when she was convinced she had been lost on them. The memory of that experience was so powerful that only the sheep and the odd car which were really details that had been inadvertently omitted when the image came into her mind, and were an integral part of it, were able to gradually reduce the desolation she felt. The experience she remembered occurred when she was still at school, and resulted from one of the enthusiasms of her then close friend Jennifer. When it was all over she had decided that their mutual interests should in future be confined to jewellery. Jennifer had persuaded her, as a result of a school sponsored walk in which the participants chose their own route and were rewarded according to its ingenuity, to accompany her on what she described as a short walk along a well-marked but seldom used path across the moor. From the very beginning Prunella could not see any indication of a footpath, but she knew Jennifer was thorough and didn't doubt that her friend could detect signs of a path whereas she, Prunella, was inexperienced and could see no sign. Prunella thought the small circular object which Jennifer had from the outset and then repeatedly placed on the ground was some device to find minerals, as on a project at school in geography they had been analysing the soil content of the moor, and found all the soil was the same. After about four hours of walking when it began to get dark, and Prunella could only see moor in every direction, she had become irritated but not alarmed because she knew if they continued to move downwards the main road would eventually be reached. When it eventually became dark, Jennifer, who had no doubt carefully timed the whole journey, had revealed that she, at the age of fourteen, smoked cigarettes, and by lighting a match could see the device which was, she explained to Prunella, a compass to give them the correct direction. When Prunella told Jennifer she did not know she smoked, Prunella's exhaustion of body and mind was increased by Jennifer accompanying the physical walk by a long ramble through various plans she had devised to subvert society. She did not permit her anger to rise above mild irritation, but listening to Jennifer she had a sense of the utter futile nature of much human activity as she wearily trod further thinking that she would collapse though sheer exhaustion before their destination was reached. In view of Jennifer's meandering discourse she was at a loss as regards accuracy in determining the flights of fancy in which Jennifer had indulged planning the walk; if there had been a choice between a long walk and a short walk no doubt in the circumstances it would have been a long walk, a very long walk, but Prunella had enough sense to comprehend that longevity and shortness was too simple for the complex machinations to which Jennifer was given; which hitherto had only involved talk that Prunella thought ridiculous, and ignored because of their common interest in jewellery.

Jennifer explained that she did not wish her smoking to be publicly known, as she intended to create a grand demonstration by smoking her head off at the school Christmas dance, to which the boys from another school were invited. Jennifer had, she said, read about the dangers to health from smoking, but it was an important form of relieving tension in an inhibited society.

Prunella was seldom given to sarcasm but she knew spades when she saw them, and although she thought the headmistress was not incapable of offering cigarettes to pupils, it was unlikely she would do so. The leisure afforded by mile after mile of moorland recalled to Prunella the occasion when the headmistress had interrupted a lesson taken by a male member of staff to ask him for some tobacco. It could have been used in some laboratory experiment, or it might in some indirect way have been a means of indicating to some of the inhibited girls, including Jennifer, that their headmistress was fighting the same enemy but on a different front. Some of the younger teachers were certainly capable of handing round the fags. As Jennifer oscillated between women's liberation and the valuable work done by the Footpath Preservation Society, the flow of rhetoric was brought to a halt by the sight of a lamp about two miles away. So at about midnight they reached an inn, The Sheepshearer, which owed its existence to the days when sheep were driven across lonely tracts of land to a market. When they reached this point further walking was thankfully avoided, after a dog barking had brought out the keeper of the pub who, not wanting a journey of hours to Andchestford and hours return in his car, had offered the girls accommodation for the night. It was all part of Jennifer's scheme, Prunella surmised, when Jennifer, who could not have seen the inn sign in the dark asked the landlord how The Sheepshearer had got its name and why it was so isolated.

She was saying to herself, "If you don't go someone else will," as she tried to recall something associated with Donald when, looking in her diary she saw that in the afternoon she had to attend the women's section of the Civic Society, whose fundamental aim was to preserve the architectural heritage of Andchestford. She remembered that Donald had made the remark to his wife at an extraordinary gathering to which all the wives had been summoned by phone calls from the office.

"I want you to be here by eleven o'clock," her husband had said about ten o'clock one morning three years ago.

As her husband had never before (or since) phoned her in such a peremptory manner, Prunella was at the office by ten twenty, when her husband remarked that Edna and Mrs Hetherington would be there soon.

"We just want you to attend a meeting of the women's section of the Civic Society this afternoon at the Corn Exchange. Knowing the difficulty Donald will have in persuading Edna to go, we thought we could impress upon her that the meeting is an activity essential to the firm. We have been informed this morning that the council intend to demolish this building. I have rung the Civic Society, and they are holding a meeting this afternoon when the proposed road will be approved by the women's section to which I have managed to get you, Mrs Hetherington and Edna invited."

"Edna?" interjected Prunella, who knew that Donald's wife had come to the conclusion that the dinner parties were as far as she would go in getting involved with 'the world the flesh and the devil'.

"Yes, Edna, whether she likes or not," replied Christopher, perceptibly raising his voice, which was as close as he had come to shouting at his wife.

Instinctively Prunella knew that a few well-chosen words were required to restore stability.

"Well, doesn't Walter know about it?"

Mr Walter was the husband of the daughter of a sister of Mrs Hetherington's and a member of the town council.

"Unfortunately, no," said Christopher.

"But surely it's of historical interest."

Christopher, on hearing his wife cut her way through the tangled growth of deceit and intrigue, thought what a remarkable woman she was; Walter's reason for being on the council was to keep the partners informed of its affairs since Prunella's father, who had been town clerk, had retired, and with the plethora of new men from all corners of the country, not Andchestford born and bred, meeting as permanent staff, presenting the various council committees with strange schemes. It was also undoubtedly true that the building, although not listed, should have been. Built just before the First World War it was opulent in mosaic, marble and wood combined so exquisitely and with appropriate symmetry indicating the mysteries of wealth, together with its exact dissection by Latham, Blakeshaw and Smithers.

When Edna arrived, Donald explained that the conspirators who had made such great progress were certain to notice the absence of the wife of one of the partners, and all that was required of any of them was to sit demurely through all the meetings of the women's section of the Civic Society indicating a friendly interest in their meetings but limiting themselves to polite conversation.

"We," he announced to all and to his wife in particular, "will do all the concomitant lobbying from this end and see that no more is heard of it, and the sooner we can get the town clerk a job with a higher salary in another place the better. We shall of course forewarn his new employers of his mercenary nature."

Prunella had noticed before that Donald adopted unusual mannerisms of speech when his wife was present, and concluded that it derived from his desire to bring extraneous matter not associated with the chapel into some sort of benign coexistence with it. Prunella, though thinking religion unnecessary, nevertheless considered its old-fashioned language charming and poetic, and was absolutely certain that Donald's unusual choice of words when his wife was present indicated his grasp of religion was basically imperfect. Her body shuddered, and she was delighted by the thought of toppling Donald from that pinnacle from which he surveyed the world. She did not wish to destroy him, but to administer a series of nasty shocks. She wished to control him, and she remembered seeing a peacock among the trees in the Arboretum. What she would like to do was pluck Donald's gaudy feathers and watch him twinge, as each one was drawn from the body.

The town clerk had soon packed his bags, the demolition

plans had long been declared a classic example of local government ridiculing the advice it received in circulars from the Department of the Environment, and the three ladies every week attended the women's section of the Civic Society. Because she thought books silly, Prunella tended more than most people to remember conversation, or in the case of the Civic Society random bits from the lectures and talks; because there was no difficulty relating any subject to those aims of a civic society, and because a meeting was held weekly, anybody who could talk about anything for twenty minutes was welcome. History occurred quite frequently, and Prunella remembered it not for its relevance, but like the moor for its feeling of desolation, rather like a person immersed in anxiety and worrying, watching people perfectly happy who are not so much indifferent to his or her problems as unaware of them; and many people have full lives in which, by the immutable laws of nature, there is little room for others. History to her was a pageant in the same category as Jennifer's present life, about which she knew nothing. She remembered one of the talks, about dinner parties when the French Regent, the Duke of Orleans, at some time in the past, had closed all the palace doors every evening so as to prevent matters of state interfering with the pleasures of the flesh . . . he had died while making love to a courtesan . . . at the same time in Britain the King, a foreigner, preferred women who could speak German, so he brought these with him from Hanover . . . she had forgotten why he did not bring his wife from Hanover . . . Mrs Hardcastle would soon be here with the post.

Prunella was just thinking that were she to get a pair of scissors, cut up her skirt towards her thigh, and assume a provocative stance at the front door she could not be seen from the road because of the rhododendron bushes, when she heard the flap close as letters were pushed into the house. Anxious to call in at the office, she quickly looked to see if there were any for the firm. She found what she was looking for.

It seemed to Prunella as she went through the oak doors and looked past the marble columns of the office foyer to the reception clerk at the far end, as if Donald was chatting up Vivien, the amply proportioned receptionist. He stood peering at her face, and was not gazing into the liquid hazel eyes which to some men promised tranquillity in their worried lives, and led others to wonder if she was the same all over. They happened to be both standing, and a stranger not aware of the austerity of Latham, Blakeshaw and Smithers would have assumed that carnal pleasures after office hours was the topic of conversation; indeed to these, Vivien's breasts with only an inch or two distant from Donald's suit, would have assumed both were about to throw discretion to the winds and go into a clinch. By the time Prunella reached them she had the situation in perspective and remembered that this scene took place every day when Donald returned from his lunch, and was quite innocent. Edna would have been proud of her husband as conscientiously doing his duty. Donald was looking at Vivien's face for signs of strain. She was not aware of his ulterior motive, and assumed that his daily attention was the customary politeness with which the partners treated all their employees. Prunella, now firmly launched in her determination to get into bed with a man other than her husband, and with a hazy impression that up till now Donald was the only man on her list, said to him when handing over the letters, "Do you come here often?" which both he and Vivien assumed referred to the efficiency of Donald as a businessman. Of course she would not have said it had anyone else been present, but Donald had never been to the Palais, and Vivien had never, in her twelve years with the firm, heard an improper remark from either the partners or their wives.

The incident which led to Donald's daily medical inspection had occurred four years ago, and on her way from the office to the meeting of the Civic Society Prunella remembered all the salacious details. It was not the salacious detail, Prunella reminded herself as she resolved to keep her feet firmly on the ground, which accounted for Donald's conduct, but his thoroughness and his ability to switch his intention between all conceivable matters with the greatest ease, and no sense of embarrassment. Some men given to a modicum of self-analysis especially if they were elders of an evangelical chapel would have ascertained signs of facial strain in a voluptuous woman by indirect means. Vivien, nondescript at the age of fifteen but looking eighteen, had been given the job of receptionist immediately she left school. Even if she had not looked older she would have probably become receptionist at fifteen, for the meticulous attention given by the partners to all their work would have made her job straightforward. Mr Hetherington had been responsible for her selection. The firm had always taken its junior staff from the town's grammar school. However, that protest at authority, of which Jennifer had been only one participant, resulted in the work 'going off'. Mr Hetherington, who had doubt that the rot would spread, said it had not reached a secondary modern of which he was governor. He would have a word with the headmaster and ensure that a competent receptionist was obtained.

Vivien never gave any cause for complaint. It was Mr Hetherington who first noticed her wan complexion during the incident which led to Donald's daily inspection. The firm was in no way paternal, and when Vivien changed from being pale to looking haggard the partners made no comment. A friend of Vivien's told Edna that the reason for her haggard appearance was that she had a bill of £700 which she could not pay. She had spent a holiday abroad with a man who said he was paying for everything, and then the girl received the bill from the hotel. Edna told her husband, and when Mr Hetherington was brought in he said if he could have the name of the hotel, its owner, and the man with whom Vivien had been on holiday, he could sort the matter out. Eventually, a business colleague of the man who was the culprit was invited by Mr Hetherington to a dinner party, and Prunella heard the senior partner ask their guest to use 'his good offices' to get the bill withdrawn. Within a week the colour began to return to Vivien's cheeks, and she was bright and cheerful again.

Prunella, who was in a scathing mood thought, 'What on earth will they do next?' as she was handed the usual summary and cup of coffee at the end of the talk at the Civic Society meeting. She had not been paying much attention to the speaker, morose over the patently obvious difficulty of seducing Donald, who seemed oblivious to sex, not even glancing down at Vivien's bulging figure which the receptionist had not restrained, though modest enough to wear a high-buttoned dress. All the more challenging, Prunella decided, for a mature man who contemplated the veiled hidden fruit of sensual exhaustion, several buttons being required for adults to undo, as they had progressed beyond the stage of the one button she had on her dress when she thrust Christopher's hand down it on the lay-by. How intoxicating to be told the room was too hot by a man who then took off his tie, telling her she too needed to feel the fresh air wafted into the room when he opened the window by the slightest degree possible. Then to reply, as if she was with her husband, in an absent-minded manner, that she could indeed do with a button being undone, and making every effort to undo it, find it too far away for her clumsy efforts. Then the man, the very model of consideration, offering his services but progressing from the top button to undo the lot. She had begun to feel quite warm.

Only hearing a word here and there as the lecturer in local history at the College of Education addressed his audience, she had the impression that he had been giving them recipes. What she thought was a reference to pickles, had been the pronunciation of pickelhaube, the traditional German military helmet up to the end of the First World War. The canopy over the platforms at the one remaining town railway station was in danger of being sold as scrap metal, he maintained, by British Railways, indifferent to the fine tracery of ironwork capped by pickelhaube in places where these had not yet fallen off. He feared, quite rightly, that were more of these points of steel to fall the structure would be announced derelict by an organization which delighted in vandalism. The other town station had seemed to vanish overnight about three years ago and astonished citizens had not yet recovered from the shock of seeing a gaping hole where the Great Central Station had stood, and were on the alert guarding other possible targets which the railway authorities might demolish to rubble, or cause to completely disappear in a day, such was the speed with which they habitually acted. He explained that the military paraphernalia was the result of the canopies being placed above the platforms when the Princess Royal, the eldest child of Queen Victoria, married Frederick, Crown Prince of Prussia.

Prunella always gave the handout to Christopher during the evening, and in sensing her listless and apathetic mood, he returned from the library with the summary of the first meeting of the Civic Society which declared 'that from the ashes of the old town, which is a Victorian monstrosity with later gimcrack additions, would arise a new town built by British architects, as illustrious as the Corbusier and Bauhaus traditions of Continental Europe. The rebuilding would be as complete as that of the village Edensor in Derbyshire by the Duke of Devonshire in the last century, but as merits this new age of white-hot technology and progressive education for all a town, a conurbation, a tantalizing phoenix of brick and concrete, and not a few houses clustered round a church, would arise. Carthago delenda est. A new Carthage would replace the old Andchestford, but the name will remain the same. So impressive will be the new town that should, in some fabled future age, a conqueror wish to raze the buildings to the ground and plough over it, he will let it stand, astonished by its form symbolizing the diverse contradictory nature of the human race'.

After he had finished reading, Prunella, unused to such monologue from her husband, who was aware that something was disturbing his wife, gazed emptily into space. Indeed he decided profound changes were taking place in Prunella, when to his question whether the talk had been interesting she replied, "It was only about cooking."

She, being perturbed that her husband should behave as he had never done before, since he was not quietly at work on a crossword, felt that some more on her part like the incident in the lay-by, but of a different kind, was called for to preserve a facade of domestic harmony. It did not take her long to remember something from a previous talk so she said, “It’s a pity our architects are not as good as our writers.”

Christopher, content at his perspicacity that Prunella was in the throes of radical change thought she was quoting from a book, and slept like a child without a care in the world, firmly convinced that Prunella’s revision of her opinion that books were silly could only be a change for the better.

CHAPTER FOUR

For those who have never visited Andchestford a precis taken from the various guides available will give some indication of the nature of this large town of a quarter of a million inhabitants. It is to the east of the Pennines, if you imagine the mountains extending further south than is actually the case, and include those hills which are high enough to be called mountains. To some it was in the Midlands, the very north of the Midlands; to others it was in the North, the very south of the North. In any event, it cannot be missed by those who refer to a map. The inhabitants could ignore the radio weather forecasts which placed them in both regions (not in the same bulletin it must be pointed out to those who think the BBC capable of anything, but such confusion was apparent to those who listened to the forecast twice in the same day). Lest it should be thought the people of Andchestford were in awe of the BBC and confined criticism to weather forecasting, which to some is no more exact than astrology, the Annan Report on the future of broadcasting, whose evidence was collected over many years, but whose conclusions of pious platitudes about the BBC recounted by the distinguished academic who was chairman of the enquiry, was described by Mr Hetherington in a talk he was invited to give to Andchestford Rotary Club as 'a load of codswallop'.

Such applause as greeted Mr Hetherington had never been heard before in living memory in Andchestford, and was unlikely to be heard again. Had Lord Annan not been the Provost of King's College London but the principal of Andchestford College of Education the opinion, 'a load of codswallop' would still have been voiced by Mr Hetherington, whose anger resulted from being a firm admirer of the BBC both in its sound and television. He was equally fervent, in a closely argued speech, in his enthusiasm for independent television. Indeed his fellow Rotarians thought his impartiality so impressive that he should have been chairman of the inquiry. The *Andchestford Courier*, the daily evening newspaper which is worth 6p of anybody's money, reported as follows: 'Mr Hetherington was of the opinion that the benefits of radio and television were considerable, and the hard work which resulted in an excellent service would not receive the attention it deserved because of the eulogistic fantasy indulged in by Lord Annan, whose remarks people would not be able to take seriously.'

The town was a product of the Industrial Revolution with ironworks, hosiery and brick quarries. Its many chapels bore witness to it having been a bastion of nonconformity. The principal Church of England place of worship was attributed to various Victorian architects; no one quite knew whether Butterworth or Scott had designed it. The lifeless bishops and saints along the west entrance gave the impression it was the work of Scott, the interior with its painted walls and intense atmosphere conveyed by low vaulting that Butterworth was responsible. The town hall was palatial in grey stone, solidly impressive, owed nothing to either the country house traditions which hitherto monopolized the construction of buildings of this size or to the Gothic revival. Large slabs of grey jutted out from either wing of the building at every other layer of stone so as to give a feeling of inconsequence, of levity, to slightly offset the huge mass of an oblong whose purpose was to convey the weighty matters discussed inside. The angles of the building had, as an ally, the flower beds which had been planted in the large expanse of lawn in front of the building. Around the grass verges was an eight-inch high looped metal railing which glinted in the sunlight, and when the sky was overcast looked the same colour as the town hall. It had been saved from the collect iron campaign of the Second World War because it was a synthetic material of which its Victorian inventor expected great developments, but which was unsuitable for melting down with other iron. A recent contributor to the Transactions of the Andchestford Archaeological, Historical and Industrial Society had compared the potential of the discarded synthetic product with that of computers, which were started by Babbage in the first half of the nineteenth century, left and not developed again until the Second World War. The Darlington and the town library were of the same period, of similar design, their high interior ceilings and spacious rooms giving an accurate impression of the carefully garnered opulence which had paid for them.

By half past eleven Friday morning while assiduously dusting and vacuum cleaning for two hours – she did all her own housework, Prunella had come to various conclusions. She must get away from it all, but be home in time that evening in order to give Christopher the closing figure of the Financial Times Index; she believed all her actions, which she now regarded as having as their focal point what she gathered was the centre of Vivien's life away from the office, would have to be approached with caution in view of Christopher's extraordinary monologue the night before, and would certainly not result in her receiving a bill for £700. She had no plan to seduce Mr Hetherington, who must have been nearer seventy than sixty, but one of Prunella's attributes was to spot clues in the manner of a great detective. She was able to find a stray nugget of gold, which had arrived on a shore across thousands of miles of water from some subterranean shelf rich in gold. In little or no time the currents of the sea would have been convulsed, not by the improbable but the impossible; the prospect of Britain going back on the gold standard would become a serious topic of conversation, and a prospect not to be discarded lightly. Such flair, common to Prunella and great detectives, also has to contend with gigantic disappointment, such is the humdrum nature of the world, the predictability of events, and the monotony of the expected. In fairness to Mr Hetherington, and other men nearer seventy than sixty, it does not behove the present narrator to indicate that men of their age do marry nubile, beautiful and young women, who are as enigmatic as the first flower of spring after a particularly hard winter of many funerals and an epidemic of influenza; but the narrator will occasionally make a concession to that fractious minority who will find fault anywhere, throwing logic to the winds and postulating arguments, quite contradictory, obviously arising from a sense of power.

Reminded of Mr Hetherington's ability to get a business colleague to use his 'good offices' with respect to Vivien, and of his artist daughter whom he firmly refused to cut off without a shilling, Prunella decided to visit the 'marsh'. The 'marsh' was the name given to the motorway restaurant by Mr Hetherington and it was about forty-five miles away from Andchestford. As thirty of those miles were on the motorway itself the 'marsh' could be reached from The Oaks in little or no time at all. Mr Hetherington had a high opinion of the architecture of the particular motorway cafe, which straddles the road on plinths and has a light and pleasant appearance which extends to the adjacent petrol pumps whose lights are at the top of thin stilts. It reminded Mr Hetherington that some contemporary structures were as impressive as buildings which dated from the year dot to 1939. It was a perfect foil to the heavy lugubrious aspect which characterized the motorway itself. Prunella, who knew Mr Hetherington often participated in what in Andchestford were great events, regarded his opinions with respect, and was sure the 'marsh' would be frequented by persons of good taste. These great events, like the affair of the concave school ceiling, had the same importance when they happened in other places. The business interests of the partners were extensive, and she and Christopher, with Mr and Mrs Hetherington, had called in at the restaurant on the way back from a social function which required their attendance in a neighbouring county.

Prunella's choice of venue for her lunch seemed to her

inevitable as she considered the great weight Mr Hetherington had in the activities of Andchestford in general, and in the matter of the concave school ceiling in particular. The parents at the primary school which Cynthia's children attended had noticed the way the school hall ceiling sagged downwards in the middle, about a year after it had been built. The school, which had other unusual features, was not at first thought to be falling down.

Knowing Mr Hetherington's interest in architecture Prunella had said, "Do you know there is a new building like the 'marsh' in Andchestford?"

She had that very afternoon been talking to Cynthia, who was worried because her children could not read as well as she had been able to at the same age at the old C of E primary school, which the new building had replaced.

"There was nothing wrong with it," Cynthia had said, referring to the old school, deeply convinced that whoever was responsible for her children's backwardness in reading were capable of creating all kinds of diversions to conceal their failure to maintain standards, including demolishing the old school and giving the new one a funny ceiling in the school hall. She said as much to Prunella.

So a curious Mr Hetherington arrived at the opinion that the ceiling at Riverside Primary was about to cave in. Walter, the firm's contact with the local council, was asked to investigate, which he did at a full meeting of that body, when the Director of Education was asked if he was aware that a ceiling in one of the schools for which he was responsible was about to fall down.

"No," he said, "but I can assure everyone present that the matter will be fully investigated."

Some people in Andchestford did not fulfil their obligations as citizens as did Mr Hetherington and Walter, and a few of these who were on the council were overheard after the meeting talking to the director.

"It will do no harm," the Director was overheard to say, "to give them an opportunity to appreciate the meaning of concave. I only hope the great event occurs during assembly when everyone is present."

The Director had known about the ceiling for some time before the meeting, had consulted specialists as to the tensile quality of the roof, who had told him it would be safe until the August holiday which was about four weeks away. The remark and the merriment and hilarity which followed the Director's remarks led Walter and others to act the same day. An extraordinary meeting of the governors of Riverside Primary was arranged for the very evening following that of the council, and the school hall placed out of bounds indefinitely. The greatest discretion was exercised as regards the Director who it was thought inadvisable to send on his way so soon after the departure of the town clerk. Thereafter he became a mere cypher, closely watched, but unsuspecting as regards his new situation. He soon came to regard himself as knowledgeable about the law as the Lord Chancellor, the Chief Justice and the Master of the Rolls, as he was asked to investigate the legal nature of the relationship between local and central government in the field of education.

Another conclusion reached by Prunella as she did the household chores was to go to the 'marsh' without a bra, but that she would be sufficiently covered by a tight but thick woollen dress. It was, it is true, very hot weather but Prunella, annoyed that her underwear was all of a kind designed to conceal curves, was thankful after resolving to dispense with such constraint to find anything suitable for the trip. It is not true that Prunella was becoming soft in the head, launched on a mental aberration in which she imagined she was seventeen again, and she would not be arrested in the restaurant as she thrust the hand of the nearest handsome male down the front of her dress. Had she been someone else and thrust a hand down her dress in the restaurant it is unlikely that she would have been arrested. Offences of this kind and other similar misdemeanours in the widest conspectus are seldom notified, and it is irrelevant to consult those people who talk and write and indeed spend most of their time in some way commenting on those deep social changes which are taking place in society; merely the prerogative of the rich has become accessible to all. That difference, which led on the one hand in the twenties to perfectly sane young girls being incarcerated in lunatic asylums for having illegitimate babies, and on the other hand led to Dorothy Sayers creating the other worldly figure of Lord Peter Wimsey, the competent amateur sleuth, to distract from the sexual licence of the privileged has now disappeared. Prunella solely wished to show off her figure to the best advantage. Neither did she think she was Vivien, nor Mrs Pailton, extremely attractive wife of a local solicitor who had run off with Mr Pailton's chief clerk. She was Prunella Latham, and as she gazed at herself in the woollen dress in the mirror she anticipated no querulous remark or uncertainty from her husband as in the fullness of time, that is, at six o'clock that day, he gazed at her thrusting breasts. He would variously think of his wife as mellowing with age or conforming to fashion. Prunella would not, however, leave the matter there, and she had no doubt in her own mind that at the appropriate moment she would either do or say something which would leave her husband bewitched in his admiration of her.

The restaurant was crowded, but Prunella saw that many of the people were just finishing their meals, so she chose a table which she would soon have to herself. Before long the majority of the people left: Prunella was now at a table by herself, and many were empty. She had finished eating and was smoking a fourth cigarette. Anyone seeing her and the evident leisure she had at her disposal, would have disassociated her from the rapid activity of the motorway. She was not wearing a stout pair of walking shoes, but her woollen dress was of that type worn by matrons of the countryside who have sensible clothes of a durable nature which ignore the vagaries of the British weather. Attempts to identify Prunella in a specific way would have proved elusive. Country attire of the plain variety is worn like a sack bag, and Prunella's dress was evidently not intended to remind people of those practical activities like the storage of wheat and potatoes, which are a vital part of the national economy. Graham Cadle who had now been looking at Prunella for some time, was reminded of a Monet painting as he took in the colours of her face; white skin, brown eyes, flaxen hair and bright red lipstick. He decided she was some rural yokel, evidently female, who had vaguely apprehended fashion advice in a magazine. In the novels of Anthony Trollope, men of significance whose source of income is not always closely analysed appear from time to time. There is no suggestion of dishonesty and no reticence as regards their appearance in the social activities of that age. Today their equivalent still seem to have time by the horns as they engage in desultory activity in suits obtained from the most expensive tailors.

"I wonder if I might trouble you," Graham Cadle said to Prunella and continued, "do you know by any chance if I've missed the turning for Sandton?"

Prunella gave her inquirer one of those flashing smiles, which some men interpret as an indication that they are home and dry, and their fate has been taken over by benevolent womankind, and that they have been relieved of any arrangements that have to be made. It is all a question of experience. Graham Cadle, who had been what can only be described as the recipient of countless alluring feminine glances, took Prunella's smile as a signal that he might pursue the conversation. The smile meant nothing else to him, cognizant as he was of the infinite exertions required of men sometimes in their efforts to appear favourable to women. Similarly women have to be equally circumspect, aware of the exacting aspect of relations with men to some of whom a smile, no matter how carefully pitched, means nothing.

Prunella replied, "It depends on which way you're travelling, north or south?"

"Oh, I see," he said sitting down, and then waiting for some time as if Prunella's answer posed difficulties of the most weighty sort. As the pause lengthened Prunella did not think that Graham Cadle was suffering from amnesia.

"South," he answered, and as Prunella had made no intervening remark decided that his chair was uncomfortable, and with studied lethargy took a diary from his pocket. Further time elapsed as he searched one pocket after another for a pen.

Eventually he asked, "Do you by any chance happen to have a pen?"

She was able to oblige. Her many casual conversations in Andchestford during or after a visit to Woolworths or on the way to the antique shop frequently resulted in a name and address being jotted down for the business of Latham, Blakeshaw and Smithers.

Graham Cadle took stock of his position, and felt Prunella's quick reply offset any embarrassing implications which might be drawn from his lengthy delay before he asked for the pen. "I was going to make a note of the route, but as you evidently know the place, it occurs to me, are you going there yourself?"

Prunella, to whom his actions were laboured, and reminiscent of an actor who has been told by his producer to stretch out a play so that it will take longer, began to connect Graham Cadle with their guest at the dinner party of that week, the actor Mr Ranville and also with her father, despite the fact that Graham Cadle was about her own age. Her father was retired and spent his time in a variety of ways, mainly gardening and reading, but could abandon an activity at any time. This gentleman, who wished to go to Sandton, seemed also to Prunella to have retired. He lacked that briskness with affairs which from a knowledge of the partners and their clients was an essential element in the attitude of those who are concerned in pertinent human endeavour of one sort or another.

By now Prunella was merely curious about Graham Cadle. She wanted him to talk. She would make the running, so she said, "Not today." The sort of remark from which diverse inferences might be drawn, but the one which comes first to mind is that if sufficient reason could be shown, a visit to Sandton contemplated at a day in the future might be brought forward to that very afternoon.

Graham Cadle took the bait. "I want someone to show me round Sandton art gallery. It's not only the pictures on view I want to see, but those for which there is no viewing space stored in attics, cellars, and sometimes in places quite separate from the gallery itself."

"If you will give me your diary," said Prunella, "I will write the name of a business colleague of my husband, who will perhaps know the curator. I'm sorry but that is as much as I can do to help."

Graham Cadle said that her help was indeed more than he hoped, and they bade each other farewell.

That evening Prunella gave the name of the business colleague in Sandton to her husband. "I think, Chris, you should ring him tomorrow."

Even later that evening Prunella asked her husband if he hadn't noticed she was different.

"The truth is I was persuaded to buy some new underwear by a man who called at the door this morning."

Christopher had occasionally in the past, before she made the patchwork quilt which caused such a great sensation and was generally considered in view of the enormous amount of time which must have been spent in making it excused further charitable endeavour, suggested various organizations which she might like to support. He was sure she had bought some new underwear in town, and he construed the remark about buying it from a man at the door that she had some time on her hands and was ready to listen to his suggestions as to how it could be occupied. Prunella intended this effect. Any thought of infidelity by Prunella, which was unlikely to occur to him, had now been placed absolutely out of the question. He thought with lewd anticipation how fortunate he was to have a wife who combined sex and wit in such perfect measure.

CHAPTER FIVE

Christopher would introduce his wife gradually to endeavour of some description in a worthwhile cause. It was upon these lines that his thoughts travelled as the weekend began on Saturday morning. He would not in any way conscript her, as he looked at the totality of that which he had embarked upon. He had, as a matter of interest, just to suggest something, and he would immediately accept her decision. He preferred, however, to look at his wife's place in the family, and in society in the broadest possible context. He had the entire morning, indeed he had the whole weekend, to probe the dilemmas which he supposed faced his wife. He had an immense and overwhelming advantage as he made his various conjectures; there was no one who would refute his logic as he proceeded from one stage to the next. He concluded that before his wife was launched into that social turmoil whose object is to help each other, they should become more involved as a family. Christopher, who could look at his problem from every conceivable direction, believed that although people were assisted by a multitude of organizations, it remained true that many people led solitary existences and the involvement of Prunella would not only benefit herself but others also, and he had never known her to have difficulty talking to anyone. She gave the impression that she had a whole armoury at her command, but would fire a few shots at intervals of years just to check that the guns and bullets were in perfect working order, the intrinsic efficiency of the militaria not requiring shots at less infrequent intervals.

He began to concentrate on the plight of his wife. She was clearly not unhappy but restive. She had been like a wild animal, he thought, whose ferocity he had tamed. He recalled with satisfaction the masterful way he had firmly but kindly dealt with her in the past; as regards particulars he recalled last night, and then remembered how he had seduced her in the lay-by, but viewed further detail of his taming of Prunella as beside the point, suffused with a warm glow by what he had already remembered. He then came to what he believed was the kernel of his wife's occasional superficial, yes, but nevertheless evident, instability. She had a remarkable memory, adroit, incisive but inoffensive conversation; such a combination of qualities demanded some explanation as to why she thought books silly. It was evidently the girls' grammar school. There must be a sound reason for Prunella not wanting to invite Jennifer to the dinner party (and he was sure of corroborative evidence which he would think of all in good time) and it must have originated in that school. It had now been amalgamated with the secondary modern, and he had no reason to suppose that the pernicious malady of the grammar school would not contaminate the secondary modern. Had they not refused to take any more girls from the grammar school in the office because of their consistent inability to add up? And was that girl receptionist not from the secondary modern, secured through the 'good offices' of Mr Hetherington? Further, was Vivien not the best receptionist the firm had ever employed? A ray of optimism shone through the bleak prospect Christopher saw before him. The trouble was that people were no longer trained to cope with adversity. Old schools, which had sometimes served communities for hundreds of years, were swept away overnight, and replaced by others at which the obligation to learn was taken off the shoulders of pupils, and they acquired information about only those things for which they had an aptitude. Nobody at the age of twelve has an aptitude to learn by heart the whole of Wordsworth's poem about daffodils, but it was to their lasting advantage that they should; the discipline acquired is essential for any serious learning apart from the pleasure of recalling the verses at an age when one was ripe for philosophic contemplation, and thought how singular it was that photographed and painted daffodils had not the fresh appearance of those in one's garden. Christopher had no doubt that the ubiquitous welfare state by doing so much for people, made them less resilient to the adversities of life. He was unreservedly without qualification in favour of the welfare state; he abhorred and detested the inefficiency and thoughtless squalor of the comprehensive system of education. Prunella's dilemma was now in its proper context. Before suggesting to his wife that she hold a coffee morning, or organize a rummage sale for her discarded underwear, they should do more together. So it was at lunchtime he suggested to Prunella that on the day following, they should all visit the ruins.

It had been years since they had visited the ruins, and it was unanimously agreed that an excursion would take place. All within a radius of fifty miles of the ruins had heard of them, and Andchestford was just within the periphery. It amazed all who lived in that circle that the other inhabitants of Britain had never heard of the ruins; Stonehenge in comparison consisted of a few odds and ends from a child's brick building kit. It was a relict of the Middle Ages. Some thought for a moment that they had stumbled across a landscape of another planet. Others that within that secluded valley the county council was experimenting in some way; the county council was apt to distribute tax and ratepayers' money in the grand style, and as they contemplated the ruined edifice they marvelled at the audacity of the council, and were of the opinion that the indignation and outrage which would follow the revelation of the ruins would be a scandal of national proportions. Some naturally took the abundance of giant columns and roofless buildings for what they were; an ecclesiastical foundation. One visitor was heard to remark at the ingenuity of its drainage system, for near the top of the hill lay the kitchen, and the soaps suds emptied after the eating utensils had been cleaned would flow along dented stone until it reached the stream several hundred yards away in the valley below. A few who had been puzzled by the defiance shown by Thomas à Becket to Henry II, were put at ease as they saw the grandeur of the combination of the temporal and spiritual, epitomized by the sheer volume of sculptured masonry. It was indeed like an ancient wonder of the world, and those who were not conversant with the history of the appropriate period were bewildered that such a magnificent structure should be in state of dilapidation.

Prunella would have known, had she been paying attention to a speaker at the Civic Society, what Mr Hetherington, who liked to get to the bottom of things, had discovered about this isolated collection of buildings in a valley (only approached along a bridle road, which was tarmacked, surrounded by dense woodland). It was, he would explain, the reason why Andchestford had as its vicars men of the cloth who were, in the sphere in which they moved, distinguished luminaries contributing learned articles to periodicals like *Theology*. He said that at the time when the abbey had been closed by Henry VIII it only had a few monks, and went on thinking it best to suppose his listeners would like to hear what he regarded as a satisfactory conclusion, although he realized that his twist at the end of his dialogue would not be satisfactory to all parties: a part of the sequestered revenues of the abbey had gone to make the living of Andchestford very lucrative for the vicar.

Donald was perplexed by this account, and pointed out to Mr Hetherington that at the time of the suppression of the monasteries Andchestford consisted of a few mud hovels. Mr Hetherington, not at all put out, referred Donald to an article in the Transactions of the Andchestford Archaeological, Historical and Industrial Society, where he said it was evident that although the bulk of the abbey revenue had gone into the royal coffers a trickle, a substantial amount, had in the most intriguing way in the nineteenth century been used to augment the income of the vicar.

The summer weather heatwave had scorched the moor along whose narrow road lay the bulk of the journey to the ruins. To Christopher as he wiped his forehead, the visit was an indication to Prunella that he would bring new interests into her life with the same certainty which the headmaster of the school the children attended could regard the payment of the Latham school fees. He was, he was sure, on the precipice of great events. All the Lathams had in the past attended state schools, and he recalled the personal anguish when the decision to send the children to a private school was made. He remembered then the immense pleasure he derived from his decision once it had been made, and had not been deterred in the least by Mr Hetherington's withering comment that 'they were all tarred with the same brush', meaning that both private and state schools suffered from educational malaise. Mr Hetherington's artist daughter, who had not completely deserted Andchestford, did about once a year visit her parents, who had decided to place their house as ever open to their daughter and the friends who accompanied her. It was after several peregrinations into the antecedents of these friends during conversation at the Hetheringtons that he formed the view that scholarship was not only in danger at the local girls' grammar school, but that a malady could be detected everywhere, even in the most select of finishing schools.

"To finish what?" he would say, and it was only Donald, who could soon master any subject, who understood the full implications of the remark. How fortunate it was that he was married to Edna, who would always remain faithful to him. What was finished at the most select schools, Donald had no doubt, was the virginity of the girls, and he dreaded to think what these pampered individuals would do to a man as they sought one diversion after another to fill their lonely hours.

Christopher contemplated the ruins, Prunella, and the children, and the ordered simplicity of his life. There was, however, a jarring note. If only he could have a little excitement; perhaps actually play golf instead of just being a member of the local club, or become a part-time soldier, or a car racing driver. He rambled at will, one idea having only the smallest coherence with the rest. Somewhat disturbed by his daydreaming as he compared Prunella's liberated breasts with those of Vivien, which had always been liberated, he sought some assurance from his wife that he was a perfectly happily married man.

"You would think," he said to her, "the county council would have a cafe or at least sell hot dogs. Think of the money required to keep the place going: the grass having to be clipped, and the buildings in such a precarious state, no doubt some of them about to collapse and requiring constant inspection."

"Absolutely correct," said Prunella, to whom the great areas of stone only reminded her of the wall in their own garden, and what she now regarded as the pointless activity of growing sweet peas to which walls were an ideal background.

CHAPTER SIX

It was autumn as Christopher travelled to work; the fallen leaves turning dull yellow and brown as if in some half-hearted protest at falling from their summer perches. He always said,"Good morning," to Vivien, and search as he might he could think of nothing to extenuate the greeting. His reflex action was to go back to the previous evening, when he and Prunella had watched an explicit sexual act on the television, which she had described as 'vital to the plot' and then added, "I'm glad the children are in bed."

What had he done to deserve such a woman, who made his home a model of domestic bliss?

He was unaware of the fact that about a fortnight ago, during a week's interval between two plays, Prunella had spent two hours in bed at the Argosy with the ticket sales clerk. The bed was there for the next production, *Madame de Pompadour*, and Prunella had bought a roll of cloth in town, which she explained to the clerk, who was the only occupant of the theatre at the time, she had brought knowing the difficulties encountered in covering settees with cloth of the correct date in period dramas. Mr Hetherington had noticed subsequently Prunella's frequent use of the word athletic, but associated it with sport; no doubt the Latham's children were being encouraged to run and swim at school to divert attention from falling academic standards. The clerk was happily married, and although he parted from Prunella in what was mutual admiration, in which each saw the other as remarkable, the incident would not occur again. The clerk was concerned that his wife might find out, and Prunella had no intention of exchanging a stockbroker whose capital was in the region of £1,000,000 for a clerk on £50 a week. Nevertheless, thrilled by the dash and flair of her seduction, and the rapturous behaviour of the clerk as he slobbered his gratitude for her marvellous naked body, she resolved to enjoy a similar experience again, but not with the clerk. She was astonished how some men deceive themselves; he behaved for half an hour after she had undressed him as if he was selling theatre tickets to the public.

Christopher had parked his car, said, "Good morning," to Vivien in the foyer, sat down in his office, rang for the mail, had it brought in by Mrs Pedston, who had been with the firm longer than he had, and all the time he was intent on some strategem or other to devise a means of bringing out a more convivial atmosphere among the employers and the employed. The small writing, as it were, was barely perceptible as he saw in bold type 'Vivien'. Perhaps he should tell her how superior she was to the other girls, indeed men, who they employed, despite their formal qualifications. He would compliment her on those qualifications she had; her smart appearance and welcoming smile which made all visitors at ease.

Further, he would reveal to her in strictest confidence that she had been responsible for averting a nervous breakdown in a client whose business went bankrupt. He had come with the intention of parting with shares which were a nest egg against those adversities which can disturb advancing years. She had been responsible for the serene composure evident on the face of the man as he left the office.

He would also be more considerate to Mrs Pedston, whose long years with the firm would not be taken for granted. He was startled by a flutter of wings as a pigeon could be heard through an open window settling on an outside gable.

He slowly apprehended the reality of the situation. Donald spoke to Vivien as much as was required. The client had saved his business and his shares due to the help of Mr Hetherington. He already treated Mrs Pedston courteously.

The office ran like a well-oiled machine, and an indiscreet remark, however innocently made, could lead to the most awkward consequences. There was the case of Mr Gilliver and Mr Sparham, who had not spoken to each other for a year; both excellent clerks, but who necessitated that the partners go to the most extreme degree to show that each was held in the same esteem by the firm. If Mr Gilliver was summoned into one of the offices of the partners, Mr Sparham's advice would be formally requested for all manner of gratuitous information of which the partners were already accurately informed. Fortunately a state of affairs had now been reached where the enmity had been reduced to in-fighting in the general office, and it was recognized that the partners treated all with equal respect. Intervention in the delicate workings of the general office was only occasionally required by the partners, and did not result from complaints of being overworked but from administering first aid to a casualty as the acrimony between Mr Gilliver and Mr Sparham caused a few others to take sides with the two men who held the most senior positions below that of the partners themselves.

No trouble had spilled over for the attention of the partners for more than a year. On that occasion Christopher on hearing raised voices had thought the rag of the local College of Education was the cause of the noise, as the general office shouted its approval of the floats as they passed in the street below. Later in the day either Mr Gilliver or Mr Sparham had told him that one of the typists insisted on going above his head and seeing him, Christopher, personally. The young woman was a proficient shorthand typist, and nobody wanted her to hand in her notice. She was accordingly given the interview she requested and complained about the excessive typing she had to do for one of the belligerents. Christopher told her how much her work was valued, and that he would personally ensure that in future it was regulated. Having sensed before the interview that whatever had caused the trouble had by now evaporated, Christopher flattered the girl, wishing to make something out of the interview for the sake of the politics of the general office; most young women, he assured Jennifer, who had the same Christian name but was not the same person as his wife's late friend, had not that conscientious approach which she had, and which had not gone unnoticed as he, before going home, had a look at all the in trays and noticed that hers was always empty at the end of the day. This did not mean the other typists were sluggish, but when she had been with them longer she would be able to tell the difference between urgent and non-urgent letters. Told in the morning that the young woman had requested an interview, Christopher had arranged it for four o'clock in the afternoon. Each time after lunch when he left his office he found Mr Gilliver and Mr Sparham earnestly engaged in amiable conversation in which Jennifer's name recurred. He gathered there was mutual agreement as to the zealous and efficient attitude Miss Calder had towards her typing duties, but that it was only natural that she should take time to settle in. As Mr Gilliver and Mr Sparham had never before, and for that matter had never since shown any signs of friendship, Christopher understood this rare phenomenon to indicate that any trouble was to all intents and purposes over, and that it arose in some way as a result of the animosity between the two men. Had there been any likelihood of the proficient Jennifer Calder giving in her notice the two men confiding in no one, but each certain of their right, would have remained stubbornly silent to the end; so Christopher having fixed the time for the interview so that passion might subside found his reason justified.

Jennifer was not only efficient but also anxious to get on, so quickly after joining the office she had placed her standard alongside that of either Mr Gilliver or Mr Sparham, and sure of her ground had let it be known that she liked Mr Gilliver and could not stand Mr Sparham, or it may have been vice versa. Her action was the result of raw inexperience, but she was equal to it. Her consequent despair of audible crying, the momentary raising of voices as her plight became known, her ready acceptance of consoling words from all and sundry enabled her to wriggle out of her allegiance to either Mr Gilliver, or it may have been to Mr Sparham, long before her interview with Christopher, and to adopt that attitude of serene composure in her work, and impartiality to all who gave her typing for which she became noted.

Christopher remembered the incident, and pressed the button, which brought Mrs Pedston into his office.

"Would you tell Miss Calder that I would like to see her."

After giving Mrs Pedston the message Christopher relaxed. How simple when you thought about it to introduce the extraordinary into the menial exigencies of office routine; an event which would take both participants, he and Jennifer Calder, onto a higher plane. Such flights of the imagination are apt to confuse the faculties of men whose experience of women is limited. It all depends on what is expected from a clandestine tryst of lovers.

"Where on earth are they?" he murmured as Mrs Pedston waited for Miss Calder to return from the toilets. What he vaguely intended, he had not acquired the requisite techniques to accomplish. His predicament was obvious as he went from the drinks cupboard to search through his desk drawer for a tape measure. He was fertile with impracticable delusions. He had lost his footing on those slopes of Latham, Blakeshaw and Smithers which he knew so well. No doubt there was a tape measure somewhere in the building, which he could stretch around Jennifer Calder's body as he explained to her that the office clothes which he proposed to obtain would have a tuck put in here and be let out there, as all would have perfect fitting garments. If his knowledge of the opposite sex had more depth then he would not have been daydreaming. The truth was, apart from his wife, the only other time he had an arm round a young woman was during his national service in the army. He went two or three times to classes in ballroom dancing arranged by contacts of the firm in the British town in which he did his army service. His entire social life outside the barracks had been spent in inconsequential chatter among the families with whom the firm had contact; the only sortie into the nightlife of the area were the dancing classes which ended at nine o'clock, and to which he was accompanied by young ladies who already had boyfriends.

Jennifer Calder knocked at the door, and simultaneously Christopher picked up a copy of the *Financial Times* from a quantity which lay on a side table.

"Please come in," and, "I will be with you in a moment."

He asked her to sit down. He was in fact ready to speak, but as he placed the newspaper on his desk Jennifer noticed it was a week old. There is no reason why back copies of the *Financial Times* should not be of interest to a stockbroker, but Jennifer had done Mrs Pedston's secretarial work when that redoubtable woman, whose age no one dare ask, had been ill for a month. Mrs Pedston was an old lady, and it was thought she might take her illness as an indication that she should retire. Jennifer had fetched and carried for Christopher during Mrs Pedston's absence, noting every detail in case Christopher should ask for something unexpectedly; she wanted to show that she could use her initiative. She therefore noticed that the copy of the *Financial Times* which Christopher placed on his desk was a week old. It is the sort of detail observed by typists who have to date the many letters they type correctly. Something, she decided, had disturbed Mr Latham's usual practice of reading that morning's edition of the *Financial Times*, but what it was she had not the remotest notion. It was, she reminisced, thinking of the previous interview which had occurred because Mr Gilliver and Mr Sparham could not get on, typical of Mr Latham's courtesy that she should be invited into the office for an ordinary talk when other more pressing matters were requiring consideration. She unhesitatingly took the view that a crisis was being successfully overcome despite obstacles. She was prepared for Christopher's remarks, and a little excited at what he might say. She did not expect promotion for there were no vacancies at the time.

"What I want you to think," said Christopher as if he was giving sound advice to any client, "is that you are an important part of this firm. I certainly don't want you to go touting for business; that is what Mr Hetherington, Mr Jones and myself are here for, but should anyone, and I leave it to you to decide whether the inquiry is serious, want advice on any financial matter, then you can give them one of these cards which has my office and home telephone numbers on it. Should they run out you have only to ask me for more. You are under no obligation to give a card to anyone, and any chance of promotion will not be affected by failure to hand out these cards. All employees, once it is considered they would like an indication of the regard for their work, are given this opportunity. In some cases it has proved a means of helping the family or friends, and we should do it for this reason alone. We would not wish any employee to think that by helping either their family or friends in this way, that they are trying to curry favour. It is the least we can do. Jennifer, would you like a drink?"

As soon as the full implications of Christopher's had sunk in, Jennifer glanced round the room to make sure there were no windows. Christopher did not yet realize that Jennifer was actually one move ahead of him. He saw himself as about to embark on a formidable infantry assault course, and expressed his intention by pouring her a tumbler full of sherry. As he turned towards the drinks cabinet he felt the most pleasant sensation below his left shoulder blade. He leaned back and experienced compressed flesh beneath both shoulder blades. More was yet to come as Jennifer flattened herself against him.

"Lock the door Chris."

He quickly found the key, while she decided that a tumbler of sherry was nothing on an adequate breakfast. No, Jennifer was not massaging his stomach but his nether parts, as he reverted to the language of crosswords in this venture outside matrimony which he had not taken before. The exchange of caresses soon became mutual. It was evident Jennifer was as involved in primitive desire just as much as he.

"Let's do it like in the pictures in the library." The town library had paintings of nymphs and satyrs on its walls. "Take off your vest." Anxious to oblige in every detail, but confused by the variety of images in his mind as he visualized the paintings in the library to which she was referring, he need not have been concerned, as he promptly complied with her next suggestion.

"Stand with your back against the wall; it will be better." He seemed to be prepared to go on all day, but she was firm that they should dress.

"Could you give me the business cards you mentioned, Mr Latham."

Within half an hour of first entering the office, she had returned to typing the correspondence. There was curiosity about the interview; the brash young woman who had so resolutely hoisted her colours alongside either those of Mr Gilliver or Mr Sparham had, after the episode of crying, turned into the ideal diplomat. She handed the business cards in turn to Mr Gilliver and Mr Sparham and both congratulated her and themselves.

Each of the men believed he had been responsible for the stable running of the office; the partnership had not found itself employing temporary staff from the employment bureau. Such was the confidential nature of their business that the partners overcame their one and only typing crisis by Donald promptly asking Edna, who had been a shorthand typist, to help out, which she did for six weeks while her husband investigated the reasons why they had the shortage of typists. So thorough was his inquiry that Mr Gilliver and Mr Sparham were individually, in the most discreet manner over a long period, enlightened by Donald about the changing attitudes regarding employment in a universal context, which just fell short of recounting the difficulties typists would have when the first settlements were made on the moon. What he said was effective. Jennifer thought how enjoyable a way to start a morning's work.

Christopher was wondering whether or not he should divorce Prunella. Donald, he knew, would have trouble with Edna, but he had yet to see Donald at a loss for explanations as he relished his recent encounter, and Donald would reassure his wife. Edna did not expect the rest of humanity to conform to her views; it was plain to all that only a minority of the population attended the services and meeting of the independent evangelical persuasion to which she belonged. She would recall that Mrs Pailton had run off with her husband's chief clerk, and other incidents which would remind her that the Latham's divorce was socially acceptable. Indeed he concluded Edna was quite capable of arriving at the abrupt conclusion that his divorce posed no niceties even for the most prudish mind. Edna had her own opinion about marriage, but as she saw the question she was one of a minority who had to fight a battle not in an unheeding world, for he understood that the congregation of the chapel was increasing, but in a world of great problems, and there she would let her beliefs rest. A great explosion had a tame ending. As for Jennifer, he was certain that if either she or he decided that there would be no sequel, so it would be. Her request for the business cards, the reversion to ordinary office routine convinced him that he was dealing with a person as astute and reliable as the most trustworthy person he was likely to come across in the everyday activity normally associated with Latham, Blakeshaw and Smithers. Finally, he could not decide whether he preferred Prunella or Jennifer.

Having dismissed any worries about his own position, he considered its advantages. His wish to chat up Vivien had been removed by his recent encounter, and although Jennifer would not be reticent about her favours he could not ask Mrs Pedston to fetch her to his office twice a day, not even once a day. If he were to get Jennifer to step into his office again in the next six months the smooth even pace of routine would be disturbed. An improper liaison would not be suspected at first, but there are many phases of favouritism short of explicit sex which had to be avoided. Consider the delicate balance that had to be maintained to assure Mr Gilliver and Mr Sparham that their services, experience, advice and breadth of knowledge on various topics was equal. With Mr Gilliver he would discuss the plays at the Argosy, and accepted Donald's opinion of the man as being on the same level as any professor of English Literature. Donald regarded

Mr Gilliver as a rare phenomenon, which was really unfair to Mr Gilliver as he was not an abstract quality as defined by the clinical analysis of Donald. Talking away from the power struggle in which he was engaged with Mr Sparham, he became in the solitude of a tête-à-tête in one of the partners' offices a warm, vibrant person whose reflections on reading or a play had a quality of expression which captured the vivacity of language. Mr Sparham was a gardener who was as familiar with an Elizabethan parterre or nineteenth-century landscaping by trees as his own garden in his semi-detached house. Christopher would discuss with him the merits of flower seeds purchased from Woolworths by Prunella. Donald would buy a book long out of print so that in his conversations the exact period flavour could be obtained. Mr Hetherington would mention to Walter, the town councillor, Mr Sparham's observations about the shortcomings of the Arboretum. What innocuous hobby could Christopher share with Jennifer, as he remembered the informal chit-chat of the office. He would be ruthless, insist on parity, and he had a springboard, as he thought, by virtue of his common enthusiasm with Fred Clayton, one of the clerks who was a university graduate, for crosswords. He would have to proceed with the greatest caution. It would be as well if he checked that Jennifer had not lost that calm which she had when she left his office. Passing Mrs Pedston's small room he could hear her typing, but had no hesitation in entering the general office to ask Mr Sparham if he knew where she was; glancing round at the same time as if to indicate to Mr Sparham that he was aware he was too busy to notice whether Mrs Pedston was or was not in the general office. He could hear Jennifer telling one of her colleagues, placing her morning cup of tea to one side, that she would have difficulty with his typing. All appeared to be in order. Mr Sparham who had seen Mrs Pedston enter her own office, wondered why Christopher had not heard her typing, but as it seemed to be one of those problems to which there is no answer at the moment, he stored it away for future rumination, suspicious at Mr Latham not quite being his usual self. Perhaps his hearing was impaired by congealed wax; in any event time would show.

Mr Sparham did not have to wait long for his curiosity to be temporarily satisfied, but he was not to suspect that the furore of consultation that took place in the afternoon between the three partners was begun by what could be described as an excerpt from a blue movie in Mr Latham's office. It is not really an accurate comparison, for a blue movie would have lasted two hours, and not only would have included Mr Sparham but also Mr Hetherington. At some point Edna would have made an entrance, and all her modesty and beliefs would have been replaced within a few minutes by a gang bang in which her rather plain face would soon be eclipsed by her other more photogenic features as her ample pulsating flesh, breasts and buttocks would be massaged and clawed and ended for a brief spell as she shrieked in the ecstasy of orgasm. The interval would have been very short and slips of female and male organs would have accompanied Edna's commentary as she examined the men to single out the most endowed. Her throbbing, lush, hairy vagina would be seen as a fit receptacle for the thickest and longest penis. Insatiable after the first encounter each penis less in size would thrust up her slit.

Christopher, intent on obtaining a regular excuse for seeing Jennifer, had decided to approach the other partners with a view to getting staff at all levels to work in a more convivial atmosphere and more involved in the external business of the firm as he thought of mating, sleeping and mating with Jennifer in an hotel in Manchester, one in which he was unknown.

As Mr Sparham observed the events which were to culminate in a few days in a new personnel strategy, he had no suspicions of the motives and results expected of the enterprise. He soon recognized that some moves were afoot after Christopher had made two or three visits down the corridor to the offices of Mr Jones and Mr Hetherington. He ascribed it at first to an intrigue on the part of Mr Gilliver, as he recalled that the detestable man had been closeted with Mr Jones for a long time about two days ago. He forgot, in his excited state of mind as he watched the comings and goings, that in what must have been within the last week Mr Hetherington had told him that the three yew trees which he suggested for an improvement in the Arboretum were being planted. Mr Sparham had always been a little suspicious of Mr Jones because of his unquenched thirst for fresh information of various kinds. To Mr Sparham the partners' arguments were a collection of valuable information, whether it concerned gardening, which was their principal mutual topic of conversation besides stocks and shares, investment, or insurance or any financial transaction, or other snippets of distilled wisdom he had overheard Mr Jones mention. It was information because it lacked any colour which he associated with his flowers and the tenor of the words of his letters to his wife from North Africa during the war. 'Distilled wisdom' was a phrase Mr Sparham had, but was too circumspect to mention to anyone about the great diversity of subjects on which Mr Jones could give his opinion; the partner had not been faulted yet, but within this phrase was a codicil portending a future possible mistake.

Occasionally Mr Sparham in one of those slack periods which all offices have, as the workload fluctuates, would wonder at the terrible consequences which would ensue if the partner once got the premises wrong on which he built his arguments. He associated Mr Jones' chapel with an evangelical kind of religion in which sudden conversions to a new way of life occurred overnight. It so happens that in the partner's case, because of his family's long connection with the chapel he was one who evangelized, and was committed to religious views on which he was unyielding. Mr Sparham, however, was not omniscient. In the doldrums of his work when he had to let his thoughts meander he was struck with a terrible fear that overnight Mr Jones might suddenly become a thoroughgoing communist; he had not as yet suggested that the trees in the Arboretum be felled and a gigantic lido be made for the enjoyment of the citizens of Andchestford. Mr Gilliver was probably conniving with Mr Jones to reorganize the desk positions in the office; it was typical of the man to ingratiate himself in this way with one of the heads of the firm. Once moved from his usual place various forms of indignity could follow, especially if that 'grub' let it be known that he had suggested the changes to Mr Jones. When inadvertently he called Mr Gilliver the 'grub', he could always salvage his position by a reference to the problems that beset gardeners.

Mr Sparham had a vague enmity towards Donald, which nearly always he forgot, but which arose when he was strongly disturbed. The office had been reorganized about six months before Jennifer had joined the firm, and so had preceded her bout of crying which had resulted from her taking sides between Mr Sparham and Mr Gilliver. Donald had decided on the reorganization, and had carried it out with his flair for stating reasons which no one found able to refute. Double glazing and larger windows would make the office warmer and lighter; heat would be saved. Mr Gilliver and Mr Sparham placed at opposite ends of the room and not both next to the door to the partners' offices would emphasize a degree of independence of the general office and its reliability. The typists, who had previously been scattered and attached to particular clerks, were placed in the centre of the room where they would be able to do all the different kinds of typing at various times and so gain more experience. Mr Sparham's objection was rooted in the belief that the partners should not intervene beyond their proper sphere; the firm did not use quills and ink wells, but to Mr Sparham the fittings should have remained as they were. He thought that the main consideration was that the work should be done, and to achieve this aim the proficiency of the staff was the only requirement. New windows in the general office would have no effect on the falling standards at the girls' grammar school which had led Mr Hetherington to use his 'good offices' with regard to the secondary modern where the rot had not yet set in. Mr Gilliver had the same outlook, but as each hated the other, there was never any possibility of them knowing they agreed. Donald had decided, and convinced Christopher and Mr Hetherington that as the two enemies were invaluable to the firm, everything reasonable should be looked at in order to prevent the situation worsening into chaos and disruption. He had not only perfectly understood who Mr Sparham meant by the 'grub', but also that Mr Gilliver in his frequent references to 'one who shall be nameless' coupled with 'horticultural wind' referred certainly to an author who he thought had gone to seed, but also to Mr Sparham who was a low form of life unable to defecate.

After Christopher had succeeded in arranging a meeting for three o'clock with the other two partners, they all met in Donald's office. Mr Hetherington tried to avoid such gatherings at a high level in his office because he did not wish to give the impression that his age in any way gave him authority over the other two, which even if given out of respect only, he wished to disclaim. Often he put forward redoubtable viewpoints which he wished treated on their own merits. The misgivings of Mr Sparham and Mr Gilliver about the reorganization of the office had been put by Mr Hetherington, who knew their innate feelings, like the most eloquent barrister pleading for his clients. Intuitively the other two apprehended when Mr Hetherington was speaking for himself, and when he indicated he was rounding off, that is looking at a question from every aspect even to the extent of explaining a rationale or attitude with which he himself did not agree. In two respects these meetings illustrated why the partnership was so powerful in face of competition from the plenitude of advice and services available in the City of London, and which many people in the regions liked to contact direct. It is known for certain that the inhabitants of Andchestford preferred to place their assets in the hands of Latham, Blakeshaw and Smithers, and this quiet confidence spread when they prospered, but heard that others had not had such reliable advice. In a word, the firm was not afraid of the City, regarded it with politeness and courtesy, but not with deference and awe. The two respects originated in the days when Mr Hetherington's father had been a partner: they consisted when any radical structural change in the firm was contemplated by one of the partners writing a memorandum after the meeting, being a concise but exact summary of the discussion with freely added points which might occur to the writer as he scribbled away, and a tradition of the use of phrases once or twice a year by Mr Hetherington and without doubt in the course of time by a successor of some apt phrase from Latin. Mr Hetherington's father had told the headmaster at the local school that he wanted his son to attempt to gain a scholarship to one of the old universities. It had meant Mr Hetherington as an adolescent writing numerous essays, and becoming adept in Latin in which a minimum skill was required whatever subject he would read at university. Mr Hetherington senior was convinced that most undergraduates at the older universities spent all their time either preparing for the boat race, or in a fashion typical of the British gentleman whose modesty was incalculable, not training for the race for which he was naturally skilled, punting nonchalantly on the river. The punting was not done for the benefit of the ordinary British citizen, for when playing with the village cricket team the young man would show him sporting prowess, but so that foreigners observing the casual dexterity with which the punt was manoeuvred should realize how unfortunate they were in Kipling's word to be 'without the law'. These young men dismissed as hypothetical the possibility that the British Empire might one day be as 'Nineveh and Tyre'.

Meanwhile, Mr Hetherington senior decided to announce what he intended from the outset, that his son would not be taking up the scholarship he had gained due to the exigencies of the family business. He had observed his essays preparing for the scholarship, how fecund they were in ideas; writing memoranda was then introduced after very important meetings of the firm. Mr Hetherington had done extremely well in his scholarship, obtaining one which had been in the past closed, available only to pupils of one of the most well-known public schools. Mr Hetherington senior acquainted his colleagues with the information, and Latham, Blakeshaw and Smithers concluded, tentatively at first, that they had got the measure of the City whose boards of one sort or another, the Court of the Bank of England, the merchant and clearing banks, and the stockbroker companies, consisted either of people who had been to the public schools and older universities, or that persons who had been to these places if they did not sit directly on boards were grey eminences wielding power from the background. Mr Hetherington senior had been determined to analyse this world in that thorough manner which was a hallmark of the Gladstonian Liberals. The great commoner, the grand old man himself, had lectured the nation on its housekeeping; it should account for every penny. Identically Mr Hetherington senior had decided to familiarize himself with the last innuendo and nuance of the alien world of the City. At a banquet held in the Town Hall, Andchestford, to celebrate the Diamond Jubilee of Queen Victoria, a director of the Bank of England had told Mr Hetherington senior of the enormous influence of the House. Mr Hetherington had at first considered the remark a platitude so obvious in Britain, that the old gentleman must be tipsy to keep repeating how powerful was the House, which he thought obvious and proper in the great democracy to which they all belonged. It was not the House of Commons to which the director kept constantly referring, as the vicar and one of the aldermen had evidently, according to the director, been members, and to Mr Hetherington senior to his certain knowledge the vicar and the alderman had never been MPs. The power of the British upper class was at its overt peak, and senility had made the director indiscreet. As the old Hetherington was of the same mould as his son he made up his mind to investigate further. The House, it turned out, was the most prestigious of the Oxford colleges; to wit Christ Church whose Latin name bestowed on it by its founder Henry VIII was Aedes Christi; the House of Christ.

As a result Hetherington's son was launched on his Oxford entrance exam Latin, so that the language of the City with all its ramifications through British society should be known from top to bottom, its most intimate incantations, as secret as those of the Klu Klux Clan, an open book to Latham, Blakeshaw and Smithers. Nearby, the whole of Andchestford was a protest against irresponsible aristocracy which pervaded all aspects of life; had not Mr Gladstone said that practically all the prime ministers he had known had been adulterers. The municipal architecture of Andchestford was a severe contrast with the buildings of the quality, gentry, nobility and aristocracy. A profligate aristocracy, old Hetherington conjectured, did not have the time for Latin scholarship; it was just the odd phrase they used. He therefore instructed his son to carefully ascertain the extent to which the language was based on learning no matter how flimsy, or whether it was incoherent flotsam and jetsam. Young Hetherington, after he joined the firm, was given wide contacts both socially and with the City for his investigation. His conclusion was that the scholarship, however kind and indulgent a view one took, was non-existent. The firm regarded the position as one in which the potentates of the financial world in the metropolis had been outflanked; combined with hard work and shrewd business acumen Latham, Blakeshaw and Smithers was unassailable. Their local base was, like the fortifications of Constantinople, impregnable; had not William Blakeshaw in the annals of Andchestford as impeccable and honourable a place as the Rothschild family in the City. In 1814 he was secretary of the Lamb and Flag public house benevolent society, when the British Rothschilds were selling government stock to provide arms against the possible resurgence of Napoleonic France. The odd Latin phrase would be thrown out very seldom by Mr Hetherington when no one else but Christopher and Donald were present. Mr Hetherington did agree with Donald about the reorganization of the office, but in stating the misgivings which he believed Mr Gilliver and Mr Sparham to have he used the expression *panem et circenses* which translated means food and entertainment and which is described as the policy of an autocratic Roman emperor who wished to keep his subjects docile. Mr Hetherington indicated that progress had been made since those ancient times, and that double glazing and improved lighting could not be used to soft soap Mr Gilliver and Mr Sparham, who had decided opinions as to the essentials of work and their own status, and would regard the innovations as an excuse for the youngsters to be diverted from their work by useless fripperies. Donald said he anticipated no difficulty because heating bills would be reduced, and the workload more evenly spread. In any event, such was the hatred between the two men that should resistance from them be expected no reasonable man could fault what was intended; they would never agree to act together.

The other partners were puzzled as to why Christopher had asked for a meeting so suddenly. He began his explanation.

"I have not spoken before about why I requested this meeting, because no quick decisions are required, and I did not want to bother either of you at an early stage. The considerable advances made in the running of the firm are a result of Herculean tasks undertaken by you individually."

Why Herculean? thought both Donald and Mr Hetherington, who were puzzled as to why this word had so inexplicably escaped from Christopher's crossword vocabulary; both resolved to listen attentively as the word meant to them that it was a sign of anxiety. Donald left it at that as he was a person who proceeded from fact to fact; Mr Hetherington went on to think about Prunella, and to him if she had any responsibility for what they were about to hear it would certainly be worth listening to. That extraordinary woman who appeared to spend her time doing nothing, and yet always hit the nail on the head, had perhaps turned her attention to the work of the firm.

"What I mean is Mr Hetherington's ability to get us reliable staff after the grammar school fiasco, and Donald's successful plan for the general office. I suggest we get all our staff more involved with us personally. As a beginning I am putting forward the idea that they should all in turn be invited to the dinner parties, and accompany us on visits in this country and even abroad. Mr Gilliver and Mr Sparham will not object but regard the change as an advance on their own status. We haven't got a social club, and the other members of staff will enjoy the social activity. I think it should be open to all after a period of one year with us."

Anticipating objections he concluded, "If anyone abuses

this opportunity to participate more fully in the firm, then it is surely not beyond our resources to deal with that difficulty when it arises."

To Donald the logic appeared faultless, and to Mr Hetherington who saw the proposal in the context of the business and commercial world both at home and overseas, where innovation was topical and trendy or reactionary depending on whether employers' moves to thwart a potential encroachment by an alien trade union bureaucracy was thought good or bad.

Donald nodded and so did Mr Hetherington who added, "We are quite content to leave the detail in your capable hands."

CHAPTER SEVEN

Winter had begun when Jennifer received her invitation to dine at the Lathams' and bring a friend. Those well versed in office paraphernalia would have said that the invitation, only four weeks after her interview in Christopher's office, would have set tongues wagging, or at the very least Mr Sparham's mental agility should have put two and two together. In truth nothing was suspected, and Christopher knew why. To everyone, except Donald, Prunella was, as far as sex and feminine charm were concerned, a sort of goddess with Christopher as her exclusive acolyte. To Mr Sparham, who had seen her shopping in Woolworths with her husband, she was more vivid than his garden at its most colourful; moreover she was evidently flesh and blood. Her bright-red lipstick, put on so carelessly that it appeared smudged, not only covered her lips but crept over slightly occasionally onto her face. Donald never told anyone that he regarded Prunella as a fool.

On the Wednesday morning of the day of the dinner party Jennifer arrived at work as usual, and when she was sure Fred Clayton could overhear told Angela, the girl next to her, that she was 'in trouble'.

Fred, who had been to university, and regarded himself as an authority not only on economics and company law, but cannabis – he was a young Liberal – said, "I hope it's not mine."

Accustomed to his remarks which included in his repertoire, "Your bra is tight today," which was about as far as he thought it advisable to go, Jennifer replied, "It's nobody else's either. You've got a dirty mind you have," which put him in a cordial mood for a subsequent part in what she intended to do that morning. Fred Clayton had no idea of what Jennifer did outside the office. That she had lost her virginity at the age of thirteen, and had only seduced one other man besides Christopher was something he did not know.

Jennifer explained in confidence to Angela the nature of her trouble. Angela thought the best course of action was for Mr Gilliver to ask Mrs Pedston to see if Mr Latham had a few minutes to spare for the distraught young woman who appeared to be so ignorant of social convention, and the easy-going attitude of the firm in such matters. Jennifer had lied to Angela, telling her that she had fallen out with her boyfriend, and so had no one to go with to the dinner party. She had quickly caught on to why members of the general office were being invited to the dinner parties, but had not let her position as the centre of attraction go to her head. She had simply avoided being dated by anyone regularly, waiting for what Chris would do next. She just fancied him and was certainly not after any status he might give her, although their one and only encounter had at the time it happened been caused by ambition, which had previously got off to such a bad start when she had nailed her colours alongside those of either Mr Gilliver or Mr Sparham.

Subsequently, she too had seen Chris and his wife shopping in town. She was pretty, but the slapdash way she put on her lipstick convinced Jennifer that she was not concerned with sex but other things. What those other things might be she did not pursue. What Chris needed was the real thing. Chris and his wife did make love as they had two children, but probably did it in their dressing gowns.

The consensus of opinion as Jennifer's eyes began to water – she had been lavish with her eye drops that morning – was that she should see Mr Latham as soon as possible. Christopher seemed to be engaged in an interminable telephone conversation which Mrs Pedston was reluctant to interrupt in view of Mr Latham's well-known preference for correspondence as opposed to the telephone, of which there was no record, and according to Mr Latham was a method of communication more often than not for those who took last minute 'botched' decisions to quote Mr Hetherington; the opinion was shared by all the partners. As he continued his telephone conversation, Mrs Pedston did not want to break in on such an important event herself. Angela assured her that Jennifer was becoming agitated and would soon be a nervous wreck. Mrs Pedston hurried quickly to see if Mr Hetherington would use his 'good offices' to secure an interview. It was, it turned out, Edna on the phone; Donald was out of the office seeing a client. Christopher, his mind fixed on the dinner party, had prolonged the conversation as he thought that he would make it absolutely clear that the comparatively new innovation was working well.

Eventually, for the third time in her life, Jennifer entered Christopher's office.

"I've fallen out with my boyfriend, and I wondered if it would be all right if I asked Fred Clayton, Chris?" she said sitting on his desk. She soon got off, but thought if anyone had come in she could be fainting and would ask for a glass of water.

"Of course," Christopher replied.

"It's my birthday today," she lied again.

"How old are you?" Christopher replied saying the first thing that came into his head.

"Nineteen. Have a rock," and she took a tube of sweets from her pocket and spilled a pile of them which were like tablets on the desk. He quickly swallowed them, and then gave her a lingering friendly squeeze. "See you tonight, Chris," and with that she left his office.

She explained to Mr Gilliver and Angela, and then to Mr Sparham who wanted to prevent another bout of crying, that Mr Latham was so human that she was able to tell him the whole story, which was that she had fallen out with her boyfriend.

"Did he ask why?" said Angela.

"No, he is too much of a gentleman, but he asked me if there was anyone in the office I should like to invite." By now she had manoeuvred herself into a position where she was gazing at Fred Clayton. "I said Fred."

"All right, Jen, but put your knickers on." A completely formal reply for him, which was further than he had dared to go before, but which he savoured as he recalled his halcyon days as a student.

Fred lived in elegant suburbia. As a Liberal he would not wish to admit the truth or otherwise of the implications of the subtitle of one of Disraeli's novels which described Britain as 'Two Nations'. For those who admire Disraeli, the leading political novelist of the Victorian era, Anthony Trollope, had a scathing opinion of his abilities, and he is satirized as Daubeny, the Conservative leader who, if unchecked, would not only steal the clothes of the Whigs, but of their successors the Liberals by introducing as a Conservative measure the disestablishment of the Church of England, a main plank in Liberal aims. Britain surely has always been more variegated, consisting of not two but as many as a hundred nations; to the foreigner it is meritorious in that it connotes a fluid society, but to the indigenous commentator it has the demerit of social barriers in the most unlikely places.

Fred accepted contemporary jargon of the privileged and underprivileged; he was in the first category and Jennifer, who he was about to collect in his car, belonged to the second as she lived in one of the rows of terraced houses which jutted out onto the moor and fortuitously created an architect's dream; escape from harmony. Jennifer and her family were traditionally Labour, but as the most vociferous spokesman of that party continually harped on the difficulties of the poor they seemed to her, and many other traditional Labour supporters, as old-fashioned. It is not a principal aim of the writer to compose a political treatise, but politics are a means at the disposal of all citizens to attempt to control part of their destiny. It is granted that Jennifer had given no thought to the fact that standards in schools were collapsing, but it was self-evident that she and her family were wealthy. The terraced house had a small yard but no garden, but improvement grants had enlarged the downstairs rooms by building on the yard, and on top of the new spacious kitchen and dining area an indoor toilet and bathroom had been made at little expense to the family. It is quite ridiculous to postulate that Jennifer and her family should be content with their house or their jobs or anything else. When the world is at one's feet then there is further choice as to what life has to offer. If Jennifer had seduced the present writer then she would no doubt have been given an historial analogy which would have been intended with dramatic accuracy to give her more confidence about her disquiet over traditional political loyalty; the rhetoric of the left is as irrelevant to Britain as the fairy-tale castles built in Bavaria by Ludwig II and which ruined his country's finances. The comparison is not with remote antiquity, but only with the recent past of the nineteenth century.

As the guests sat down, to three of them it was an exciting occasion. Jennifer could enjoy Christopher's company and he hers. All his efforts to get Prunella to attend the luncheons of the Business and Professional Women of Andchestford had failed, as he pursued his conviction that his wife desired outlets for her new maturity illustrated by her change of underwear.

"It would be like touting for business," she had said, "and I am neither a business or professional woman."

That suggestion was knocked firmly on the head. Mulling over her reply a week later he was certain he had the answer. His encounter with Jennifer had convinced him that he was a force to be reckoned with by women in general. She was not a viper after money, but as he recalled a phrase of Mr Hetherington's about the sex education at the grammar school and which was now part of some immense comprehensive, only interested in 'slap and tickle'; but, he reassured himself, 'slap and tickle' of the widest interpretation as he looked at some of the films in the evening paper which could be seen in the town. Nevertheless, in reality he was as cautious as ever with Prunella, which objectively was perfectly natural as his now uninhibited venereal enthusiasm was begun by her. The answer Christopher believed he had hit on was to get his wife involved in some practical activity. As if half convinced, he plucked from his crossword vocabulary empirical and pragmatic. His idea did not comply with the Prunella he had known for so long, but it was evident she had changed. He asked her to consider helping out with the meals on wheels service, which in Andchestford, thanks to Walter's assiduity in keeping down the rates, was run on a voluntary basis.

"It would be a vote of no confidence in Walter," she replied with that accuracy of repartee which Mr Hetherington saw as remarkable, and Donald asinine.

Prunella had been thinking about men in a casual rambling fashion. She did not want to be picked up on the motorway or any other place by someone she did not know. Her two hours of unbridled lust with the sales office clerk at the Argosy had satiated her body, and she craved for an excitement beyond undressing men. Indeed, she believed she could undress all and sundry, and in a sort of torpor of being at a loss, and in a cul-de-sac she had a nagging doubt that she knew someone who she could not undress. Her mind had become an assortment of fragments pitted against an intellect which she had not yet apprehended, but which she realized she had no hope. Her melancholy was dispelled when she identified her inferiority with an alien mode of behaviour which at last took shape as she saw Edna's features. She most definitely had no desire to undress Edna, and her mind relaxed into languid satisfaction as she contemplated her success to date.

It was not because of any enmity towards Edna that she wished to divest Donald of his clothes, and his trousers in particular. Edna, a friendly acquaintance, had no connection in Prunella's assessment with her husband Donald. Indifferent to Donald's silences at her remarks in the past she had had no animosity towards him; but now she remembered the slight creases in his face which she quite rightly equated with sneers when she made a remark. He must be taken down a peg or two and she visualized the two mating butterflies being eaten by the bird.

"Now, tell me," Edna said to Jennifer, "just what you do in the office."

"Oh, anything which wants typing. There's a lot of variety, although I have not yet reached the stage of advising clients which shares to buy."

"But you will," said Donald, who had become convinced that there were no limits to Christopher's plan of involving the staff. He could not see it progressing beyond the stage of picking up the phone and saying, "Don't sell, we will ring you back." In the crises that from time to time shook the City, it was vital to have every available person to answer phone calls. If Mr Hetherington hadn't said a few words to put the matter in its correct perspective, Donald's keen brain would soon have done so. "We don't expect you to recommend certain shares to your friends, but if you think you can do them a good turn by acting as a go-between, one of the three of us will do our best."

"You are all so efficient," said Prunella, "that if I were to do a little filing" – she paused looking at her fingernails – "everything would get into a mess."

An ideal opportunity, Donald thought, to make it widely known that she was a parasite.

Christopher said nothing from habit; his decisions with regard to Prunella, such as how many presents to give her in a year, took at least a week to form.

"I've done it," said Edna ignoring the fact that she had been a typist, but as she had started the conversation realized she should say something positive.

"I'm a postwoman already," said Prunella, referring to the mail she sometimes delivered in the afternoon depending on what sort of mood she was in, "and I should like to see what happens to some of them."

She has a mind like a child, Donald sneered to himself, and Prunella saw the first perceptible crease line on his face.

To Mr Hetherington, Prunella had gained her objective with great delicacy. She would give Mr Gilliver and Mr Sparham something to look at, and Prunella was a sensible woman who would be sure that the filing reached the exact place for which it was intended.

"It's a good idea," he murmured to Christopher.

"So it is," said Donald, who was looking forward to the vast amusement Prunella's inept filing would cause.

"I don't know why I never thought of it myself," said Christopher; happily married men are supposed to anticipate their wives' plans.

Jennifer was liable to make quick decisions: like nailing her colours alongside those of Mr Gilliver and Mr Sparham, and seducing Christopher. Many young women would have simply done their typing and confined bold action to their leisure hours. The firm of Latham, Blakeshaw and Smithers, or its partners, was involved in the affairs of the town in a variety of ways. Jennifer's father had met Mr Hetherington about once a year when that partner, in his capacity as president of the Minster Street Liberal Club, would give an annual address to the committee. Mr Hetherington took the job because at the time he still voted Liberal, and indeed until 1945 the town's two MPs were Liberals, albeit National Liberals, and so closely associated with the National government of Ramsay MacDonald and Stanley Baldwin. Mr Hetherington had declined to be nominated about ten years ago, when the partners as a whole decided to become Conservative. Mr Hetherington had begun to see his presidency as an anachronism as the few members of the Club who did not vote Labour were voting Conservative. Mr Hetherington had, before the meeting at which he declined re-nomination, said that he intended to vote Conservative in future, and that being the case he would hardly be the President of a Liberal Club. He explained that the Socialist victory in the general election meant that all energies should be directed with the main opposition, and not a sideshow; the Liberal Party, he explained, was much too vague on education. The committee agreed that not only would they not press Mr Hetherington to stand, but nearly all believed his reasoning to be sound so that each determined without fuss or bother to quietly vote Conservative in future. The ward in which Minster Street Liberal Club stands thereafter always returned a Conservative to the town council. The Labour Party refused to seriously analyse its loss of this ward of predominantly terraced houses. Their local chairman, a lecturer at the College of Education, gave the one and only explanation, which was clearly at variance with the electoral roll which showed practically no change in the occupants of the houses before and after the loss of the ward. He said it was due to capitalists who had begun to live in the ward taking advantage of improvement grants; after the house had been improved they would sell and make a quick profit.

For the benefit of a colleague on his executive committee, who had recently graduated from a university notorious for his sit-ins, he coined the expression the 'bathroom syndrome'. Jennifer's father, who had respected Mr Hetherington over many years, had told her when she obtained the job with the firm to behave just as she would at home. Her bold confidence at the very beginning of her employment was a result of her father's advice. Since then much water had flowed under the bridge, and her confidence now had a different base.

The quick decision Jennifer now made at the dinner party was to show Fred Clayton that she was not as daft as she looked. She had to find a topic to discuss. She saw the moor stretching up the hillside beyond their house; its endless expanse written off as regards any kind of activity except for the tiny flocks of sheep.

"I go to the cinema a lot," she said to Mrs Hetherington.

"I did once," was the reply. "I went every night of the week except Sunday. I used to play a piano while the silent films were showing of course, when the talkies came in I became redundant. If I hadn't played I should never have married George. His brother played the violin, and I the piano in a jazz band. We worked hard and played hard in those days, my dear."

"I like to see a good film in technicolour, which is another change. I saw a film last week which has made me alter my opinion about the moor, which is such a lonely place. It was Italian, so romantic, as a coach was driven fast across a heath, which was blooming with sprays of purple flowers."

"*The Leopard*," said Fred Clayton, anxious to get in on the conversation, and completely certain it was safe to make a disparaging comment. "About a bunch of aristocrats, leeches worse than the Mafia."

"I'll take George to see it, and decide who's right. I withhold my opinion. Films are complex Mr Clayton, and the beautiful description given by Miss Calder may indicate there's more to it than meets the eye."

Donald, who each week received a list of films with explanatory notes from the town's advice bureau, in the event of clients from outside Andchestford having time to spare informed them that the film was from a book by Giuseppe Di Lampedusa.

Fred Clayton, who did not so much like being argued against, but regarded what he said as *ex cathedra* was taken off balance.

"Go and see an Italian film about life Jennifer," he said.

Prunella, who sensed the controlled vehemence of his remark, interposed, "And what would that be, Mr Clayton?"

"Fellini's *Casanova*," came the reply.

Mr Hetherington, who had been asked by Walter, who sat on the old town Watch Committee which could refuse a certificate for films, how he should decide and been told to vote to licence everything, reckoned that oil needed pouring on troubled waters. "That is a film about which there will be a lot of disagreement." He had seen clips from it on the television. "Some will say it's a brilliant work of art, others pornography."

"By the way," said Christopher to Fred Clayton as Mr Hetherington's remarks drew the topic of films to a close, "have you finished today's crossword in the *Financial Times*? I've two words missing." Fred Clayton had the requisite information. “I’m sure Fred would agree,” Christopher continued, “that crossword puzzles sharpen the mind.”

“Not only that, Mr Latham,” said Fred Clayton, who was now back on an even keel, “but the clues and answer provide avenues of further research into many topics.”

“You have made a convert,” said Prunella. “Christopher has never been able to convince me why he spends so many hours on what has until now been a closed door.”

Twenty-seven persons comprised the staff of Latham, Blakeshaw and Smithers. Each partner had a secretary, and there were twelve male clerks, six typists, and a filing clerk in the general office. In addition there was the receptionist and switchboard operator who also watched the telex for incoming messages. Telex messages being sent from the firm were usually tapped out by one or other of the partners’ secretaries. Mr Gilliver and Mr Sparham besides the partners could sign letters; many years ago now it had been settled that they should lose their old titles of senior clerks and be called office managers. On that occasion Mr Gilliver and Mr Sparham had made no objection to moving with the times. Between the dinner party, when it was agreed that she should help out with the filing, and Prunella’s first day at the office, over a week elapsed. She wanted Christopher to thoroughly accustom himself to what she had suggested; admittedly he did not demur, but it had been presented to him as a fait accompli. He took time with any alteration in their basic routine as husband and wife to look at all the arguments for and against the proposed change. Prunella could hit on no possible objection he might have, but still granted him the time. Christopher was relieved that events had coincided most happily so that he no longer had the seemingly impossible task of finding a solution to that lack of activity which bedevilled her life when he was away from her at the office; his infatuation for Jennifer had now spilled over like a mighty flood into his relationship with his wife, who he was convinced, along with most of womankind – although there must be exceptions like discouraging an investor to buy ICI shares which he had never as yet done – adored him. His wife only wanted to be near him as much as possible. She would not in the least be an encumbrance to him as regards Jennifer, as the next move he planned was to whisk her away to an hotel in Manchester, or some other place he had yet to decide. He had been alarmed one morning as he drove to work that he would have to take Mrs Pedston on the trip, because Jennifer probably did not do shorthand. On examining her employment application form, he found that she had done a course in shorthand. Having the scepticism of Mr Hetherington as regards courses, he saw the unknown quantity of Jennifer as regards shorthand as a challenge in which all obstacles could be surmounted. He would find out exactly how proficient she was either in the train or the car, and if he had to he would make his own notes.

Prunella's impending arrival at the office had induced in Donald a facetious remark at the dinner party intervening between the one at which it had been decided she should help out and her starting date. The crease became a furrow when he made the remark, and had not Prunella learned that creases on Donald's face were a result of her not being able to say or do anything of which he approved, she would not have pondered over his remark. It took her a whole day before she understood Donald's sarcasm. He had come up to Christopher before the dinner party began and said that he wanted his opinion the next morning on some flour shares. Not only did furrows appear, but Donald's eyes seemed to recede into their sockets; it was as if a lighting apparatus had shown up all his features except round his eyes, which were encased in black. He would never, Prunella concluded, have looked like that if he had been talking about buying shares, or about Mr Gilliver whose hostility towards Mr Sparham caused no inconvenience which was not well under control. He had, she was certain, spoken about flour to indicate to himself that she would be as useless to the firm as Mr Gilliver was valuable; he could not wait for the fun to begin.

Meanwhile, in the Jones' household the weekend before the

day when Prunella was due to start, Edna noticed on Saturday afternoon that Donald was not reading, as he normally did for two hours: it was seldom fiction, although he would read novels if he thought he should be au fait with a new trend in literature. The sudden disappearance of a London stockbrokers, which was of high repute and which declared itself insolvent overnight, had convinced him that there was more to the situation than met the eye. His determination to find the real cause for the closure led him to read science fiction books for six months, after he discovered from the gossip that followed the overnight liquidation that the stockbroker who had the most weight in the unfortunate firm had shown no anxiety, and had developed a keen interest in the possibilities of space exploration after which he was very verbose at the time of the collapse of his firm. Donald obtained from Andchestford municipal library a list of reviews in newspapers and periodicals of all the science fact and fiction books on the solar system and beyond that had appeared a year before the liquidation. His conclusion was that the man was a fifth columnist whose decision to shut up shop coincided with a review in a fashionable weekly magazine, which was compulsory reading for the jet set and all its hangers-on and lick-spittles, of a novel which was an allegory forecasting the imminent end of the capitalist system. Christopher and Mr Hetherington were told by Donald what he had discovered, and a quiet word was had here and there so that the business world as a whole became conversant with the real explanation of the last chapter of a firm which had been esteemed for decades.

Mr Hetherington, a man not given to profuse congratulation, believed that Donald's efforts were on a par with those of his own father, which had led to the actual significance of the word 'House' being understood. "It's an isolated case, Donald, but it had everyone worried. The man was respected, and loss of confidence could have happened. Use the odd French phrase every now and then. I will set the ball rolling with agent provocateur."

Edna was puzzled by Donald not being engrossed in a book

on industrial archaeology, which was his current topic.

"Why aren't you reading?" said Edna, who had recently been persuaded by her husband to add a few books on the Dead Sea Scrolls to the Bible and the concordance. This concession to the world had only been made by Edna after much persuasion. "We never read the Apocrypha."

"Not officially," countered Donald, "but we know what's in it, and the absolute truth of the gospel is illustrated by comparison. The divine revelation can never be in doubt as contradicted."

Edna was therefore reading about these ancient parchments discovered in a cave. Roughly of the same date as the life of Christ, they show the religious ferment of the time, and its authors, who were of the Jewish faith, seem to have had some form of rudimentary monastic life like itinerant friars. Edna's observation was that the authors of these old documents reminded her of the vicar and the trouble he was causing his parishioners with changes in services. Members of independent evangelical chapels are always cognizant of any change in all Church of England services within about thirty miles radius of their own place of worship, intent in showing proper charity in the event of vicars, rectors, priests-in-charge and curates apprehending the true gospel.

Thinking Donald was not reading in order to discuss the Dead Sea Scrolls, she commented, "Instead of so much concern of their own rules, they should have been preaching."

"Exactly so Edna. I told you it would only emphasize how right we are at the chapel to follow the example of Christ's ministry." After looking into thin air for another half hour Donald said to his wife, "Why I'm not reading this afternoon is because I'm thinking about Prunella. I know she will be supervised, but perhaps there may be something I haven't thought of."

"There's no need to worry about Prunella. She's very sensible."

Donald, who found people normally able to follow his precise logic, wondered why everyone did not agree with him about Christopher's wife. By teatime he had the answer; she had never done any real work and her shortcomings would be obvious as she worked with Arthur. Arthur was the filing clerk who had shown himself reliable, and who would, if he stayed with the firm, become an accountant.

Except for Donald, Prunella's impending arrival caused no similar meditation among any of the staff of Latham, Blakeshaw and Smithers. Arthur, who was only sixteen, somewhat daunted at the prospect of having to instruct Mr Latham's wife, was assured he would have no difficulty as she was the friendliest of persons, and would make no errors provided she was told exactly how to do the filing. He was given some historical background; Edna, Mr Jones' wife, had assisted in the past with the typing and there had been no fuss or bother.

"A handsome woman," said Mr Gilliver within earshot of Mr Sparham.

"Treat her like a plant," said Mr Sparham so that Mr Gilliver could hear.

Each was concerned to have no open eruption of hostilities, and both still remembered the last time a new member of staff, Jennifer, had caused a disturbance of massive proportions on account of unfurling her colours in the feud between the two. Not that it was expected that Mrs Latham would break down in a bout of crying, but desultory shooting between the two men continued, and they wanted no junior member of staff to suppose that Mr Latham's wife would become involved in their quarrel.

Those who have never worked in a general office would be puzzled by Mr Sparham's advice to regard Prunella as a plant. It was perfectly understood by those to whom it was said, and referred to the fragmentation that occurs in many offices; small groups not always related to the extent of co-operation required by the workload from each in a social way independent of others. Thus, except for queries arising out of their typing Jennifer and Angela confined their talk to each other. There were several small potted flowers in the office, which as they were there because of Mrs Pedston, had no connection with the ongoing conflict between Mr Gilliver and Mr Sparham. All Mr Sparham meant was that Arthur should treat Prunella as the rawest school leaver, whom he could mould in his own fashion. Mrs Pedston and the potted flowers had been there longer even than Mr Sparham and Mr Gilliver, and were the folklore element in the firm, which constituted one of the few matters on which they agreed. The subject of this unexpected concord was the period of time, independently assessed by the two when employees should be told the intriguing story of Mrs Pedston's flowers: people were told after about ten years' employment with the firm. Most assumed until then that Mrs Pedston brought the plants in view of one of the belligerents being an avid gardener as a gesture to others to consider themselves above the conflict or that it was beneath them. Mrs Pedston had been given her job by Mr Hetherington's father; she had come from a small village about fifteen miles from Andchestford. So diligent was she in her office responsibilities that Mr Hetherington senior had asked her if there was any way he could show his appreciation of her hard work. She had simply asked him if he would let her grow a small white flower in the office, as it would remind her of the white rose her mother grew inside their cottage. Mr Hetherington was happy to grant her request. It appeared that as long as Mrs Pedston could remember, her mother had grown white roses, and insisted that when one withered away from old age it should be replaced by another of the same colour. Old Mr Hetherington was fascinated, and resolved to find out about the white rose. He was successful and told Mrs Pedston. It was an expression of village unity. The Pedstons were Primitive Methodists, but they did not want their beliefs to cause that disruption that had followed the strife between the Established Church and Nonconformists in the Civil War, leading to the execution of Charles I, a martyr in the Church of England calendar for two hundred years. In the interests of harmony Mrs Pedston's mother had a small trellis inside the kitchen, up which she grew the white Stuart rose.

Arthur was at first thrown into confusion by Fred Clayton's appraisal of Prunella which he thought best to repeat away from prying ears in the toilet.

"She's a doll, Arthur, don't let that red lipstick think you can knock her off. Only a doll like all the junk she collects. Painted like all the jewellery she brings which nobody wants. She's not flesh and blood."

Fred Clayton had a mental dossier on Prunella, as he had on other important people with whom he came into contact. Arthur, to whom Fred seemed all talk, was soon back with his feet planted firmly on the ground, and gave him that rapt attention which he expected. Arthur's unblinking stare, with no comment, fastened straight on to Fred's view of how he expected to be listened to by the junior; to treat the junior member of the office as an equal, but paradoxically not want him to say anything.

CHAPTER EIGHT

Like all new members of staff, Prunella was officially introduced to each member of the general office in turn with the remark she was to be regarded in the same way as Mrs Jones had been, an ordinary member of the staff. Phrases like 'a valuable member in due course of a fine team', was not part of the vocabulary of Latham, Blakeshaw and Smithers as personified either by Mr Gilliver or Mr Sparham or any other person for that matter in the firm. Mr Gilliver and Mr Sparham took turns in introducing fresh members of staff. This format was long established, and obviously by treating the two office managers as equal offended neither. There was no pretence at Latham, Blakeshaw and Smithers; the fulsome language of personnel departments about teams and common objectives was not so much avoided, as not used, the work done by the partners and staff was described in a positive manner with descriptions approximately as far as human fallibility will allow with actual conditions. The subject had been fully discussed on the initiative of Mr Hetherington who, although in complete agreement with the reorganization of the office carried out by Donald, wanted to pre-empt any attempt to introduce a personnel officer. He realized both Donald and Christopher were against a project which they all considered a waste of money and an insult to people's intelligence, when they were described as doing the same job in a team, complete propaganda; it was patently obvious that all had important responsibilities but of varying degree. Mr Hetherington was in fact slightly afraid of Donald's enthusiasm for investigating subjects of the most disparate kind, and although he knew Donald was against having a personnel officer, nevertheless the firm's policy should he thought be made clear between the three of them in the most formal and official way. A meeting was arranged in Christopher's office, and the germ of it was an unfounded suspicion which Mr Hetherington would have admitted had no base, but an impartial person would have conceded that caution is the better part of valour, that Donald might put on his reading list books about personnel officers and that he would consequently present them with some kind of scheme.

"It's all bilge which no one believes," Mr Hetherington told his colleagues, and went on in that style which had caused so much applause at the Rotary Club meeting when he had denounced Lord Annan. "Everybody's got the vote, nearly everybody has been christened; each is a child of God and an inheritor of the Kingdom of Heaven."

The peroration although not essential, as the partners were agreed in describing the subject of their meeting as a waste of money and propaganda, Donald was impressed with Mr Hetherington's quotation from the liturgy of the Church of England as he was a lapsed Nonconformist. Donald afterwards explained to Edna that Coverdale's translation of the psalms had even, incredulous as it might appear, influenced the Church of England, so great was the spiritual power of the translator both in words and as a person.

After the introductions Prunella spoke to no one else all that day except Arthur. His father was a knitter in the hosiery trade, as was his girlfriend's father. In the very best of circles young women are sent to finishing schools; at the same time during holiday as during term, such is the ingenuity of those who consider themselves at the apex of the social system, their virginity ends. In the nations' state schools promiscuity is rife; each year the pregnant girl record is broken. Fourteen-year-old children are told the horrors of syphilis and gonorrhoea either on a television broadcast for schools or in class. Arthur and his girlfriend belonged to that sizeable chunk of adolescents who believe marriage is for the procreation of children, and there would be no consummation, or much necking and petting, kissing and cuddling, until after the church service which the prayer book likens to that mystery which is betwixt Christ and the Church, and which He himself blessed as a guest at the marriage at Cana in Galilee; finally there is the solemn exhortation that 'those whom God have joined together let no man put asunder'. Of course, Arthur and his girlfriend might be married in a chapel, but their outlook would be the same. The point being made is that as regards intercourse their views were traditional. Some will be amazed as to how they spent their time, but to the two young people life presented a series of hurdles whose challenge must be met. In an article in the *Daily Telegraph* it was stated that when the wealth tax was passed its provisions could easily be evaded. Arthur in his way was as skilled as any potential evader of that once proposed tax. He was encouraged in his boldness in making sensible decisions by that steady appraisal of one fact after another which was the way the firm conducted its business. The Andchestford, Wyham, Sudhampstead and General Building Society had refused over the years to shorten its title. Old Mr Hetherington, who had been a director, used to say the inclusion of the three towns and then the country as a whole indicated that all requests would be examined on their merits. Although Arthur was on a comparatively low salary, and would be when he became articled, his girlfriend, as a hosiery overlocker was earning more money than she knew what to do with. Consequently, on her earnings a mortgage had been taken out, at Arthur's suggestion, in her father's name as she was legally under age, as a mortgagee on one of those fine Victorian or Edwardian villas, which have names like Gladstone Villas or Moor View, and which the ignorant confuse with the more prolific and smaller normal terraced house. These villas with their adequate interior space are either found in two or as a terrace. The occupants of Moor View would have to be given six months' notice under the contract devised by Arthur. The house when purchased was empty and had no sitting tenants.

Arthur, whose girlfriend, considered passionate, and whose advances inch by inch after they had been to the cinema to see a particularly sexy film became more confident, was always stopped by her saying if he didn't control himself she would scream. She had noticed, nay, felt his hand placed nearer her breasts as time went by, his hand at the start of their petting was six inches further than it would have been had they not seen the film, and would have normally taken half an hour of caresses on the sofa to reach that position. She was quite decided in her opinion to keep the slightest intimacy until they were married, and Arthur agreed but he thought it as well to let himself go every so often so that she would not think he was losing interest.

Arthur found Mrs Latham most attentive, and as the filing was a simple alphabetical one, both for correspondence and the separate companies file, the task was straightforward. There was some typing, which as it was very elementary, was soon mastered; new issues of either ordinary shares or secured or unsecured loan stock, rights issues and miscellaneous information such as who now had a controlling interest, was typed on the company sheets in the index from cards handed to Arthur by Fred Clayton. As the days became a week Arthur was sufficiently analytical of himself to realize that although Mrs Latham had got all it takes, an attractive face and body, he did not have the same attitude to her as he had towards his girlfriend. She was certainly not a plant, nor for that matter porcelain of which her ultra-white skin for a time reminded him. As he noticed her lips with the smudged lipstick she appeared like a fairy.

In the evening, giving her his full attention, he visualized Mr Latham's semen running down his wife's leg. No man could possibly time ejaculation very accurately with such an ethereal creature. Indeed semen, whether his own or Mr Latham's, and whether ejaculation was premature or not appeared somehow to him to defile Prunella.

Arthur's desk was at the far end of the office, with the

occupants of the other eighteen in three rows of six facing away from him. By Friday afternoon of the first week it was as if Prunella had always been there. One or two of the junior staff who had not long left school and connected authority with nebulous instructions – such is the parlous state of our educational system – and who were slowly being broken in to that fastidious attention to detail for which Latham, Blakeshaw and Smithers is known both at home and abroad, were amazed to learn from Arthur that the boss' wife never made a mistake; a typing error would cause her to get a completely new card and retype not only the addition but all the items previously listed.

"You never know," she told Arthur, "who might see. First impressions are important with some people. We both know that a typing error properly rubbed out will not make the firm inefficient, but it's what other people might think."

Arthur, who was of the same opinion himself, was delighted to find she agreed. If she had been of a different opinion he would never have expressed his own view. His attitude to the situation was that the partners would have never let anyone, even their wives, loose to create havoc with the files.

Donald's reticence arose from his determination, after assembling positive evidence for Christopher and Mr Hetherington, to make it clear that the firm could not afford to indulge Prunella's whims and fancies. He had even got as far as formulating his case, and in particular how it should be done to preserve the Latham's domestic harmony. He regarded himself as equal to the situation and any eventuality which might occur. After he had the evidence he was quite certain that Christopher would comply with his suggestion for the sake of the firm, and he anticipated no objection from Mr Hetherington because of the hard undeniable proof he would have. He intended, after Prunella had amassed a pile of mistakes, to suggest that the least embarrassing course of action was to promote her. He would have a word with Mr Gilliver and Mr Sparham to ensure that it was known in the general office that it was the only method in a very delicate situation that the brain of man could devise to extricate the firm from the difficulties posed by Prunella not being able to master the most simple of the office tasks. He intended to propose that she should work alongside his secretary, Mrs Redshaw, for three months, at the end of which time he would think of something else to get her back amongst her twenties' furniture and bric-a-brac, and Victorian garden. She and Mrs Redshaw would be in the letters office. Each of the partners' secretaries had their own office. At least he could stop the rot from spreading, as he remembered Mrs Redshaw's habit of spraying her room with what she described as insecticide, but what had once been air freshener with a distinct scented aroma. What had made Mrs Redshaw change from air freshener to insecticide was a fear one evening, as she pondered about Donald in the quiet of her own home, that she might lose her job. He, however had never suspected any carnal intention by Mrs Redshaw, and indeed she had none, and considered the air freshener as a womanly gesture which would make for a convivial atmosphere in which to work. Donald, who was used to smelling, albeit only a sniff on occasions, various types of aftershave lotion on numerous male clients and business colleagues of the firm, never attached to Mrs Redshaw's air freshener any ulterior motive.

Arthur was completely at ease with Prunella and told her he was looking forward to the weekend, and a ride on a stretch of railway track which had been bought by a private company on which to run steam trains. In the blitzkreig which had led to the sudden disappearance of Andchestford's Great Central Station, in the haste to press on to yet more targets, some stretches of track out in the countryside had not been torn up. Prunella replied that she was sure her husband and the children would enjoy a trip, and he must give her full details on Monday.

As they drove home, Christopher asked Prunella if she had enjoyed her first week.

"I only wish I had thought of it before. Now I know why Edna is such a support to Donald."

"I don't want you to continue for that reason alone. The essential thing is that you should be happy. All three of us have now been with the firm for so long that we are able to make important investment decisions with the same ease as the tea lady makes our refreshment, and we don't doubt that the dividends will be as good as the tea."

"I've got more sense than to give my advice on the main business of the office, about which I know nothing, but Arthur's happy with a little company. He's quite isolated right at the back, and I've got nothing to think about till the garden wants doing in the spring."

There was no need for further discussion. Christopher hadn't anticipated any problems once he was convinced that his wife had hit on the answer to the tedium of spending a lot of time at home. The children obviously required less supervision as they were older. His mind was like a deep trough concentrated on a single objective which, because it was so profound, was long past the stage where the one aim required constant deliberation; he simply wanted to spend a night in bed with Jennifer in Manchester. He had selected that city because it was large, not too far away, and they did little business there so he was less likely to be recognized. Perhaps, he mused, he had saved Prunella by his ready agreement that she should work at the office, from drink, which was the only misdemeanour that entered that capacious mental trough, but recollecting those who had taken to drink he erased Prunella from this category. He reinstated her collecting, care of the garden, journeys to the office with the post, and her dutiful attendance at meetings of the Civic Society as worthy and laudable pursuits. What she had desired was more variety, and with her usual clarity had picked an appropriate choice, which had never occurred to him. How right he had been to seduce her in the lay-by, and how bold to take the bull by the horns when she was only seventeen and all his competition in the Young Farmers' Club had held back because of her age. His account of events was completely false as many members of the Young Farmers' Club had contrived to entice Prunella not only into lay-bys but haylofts, farmhouse lounges and even toilets. When the loyal toast was made at the annual dinner it was not the monarch they were thinking of but a few of the young ladies scattered among the tables whose regalia was to have obliged all as frequently as they had been requested. Christopher was not an authority on the moves of the age to which Mr Hetherington assured some despairing fathers at the Rotary Club there would be reaction as the pendulum of history swung backwards and forwards.

The following Monday Prunella, who was just old enough to remember steam engines, asked Arthur the extent of the line, and learned it was about five miles long.

"It's a pity," she said, "the track into the town has gone, otherwise they could make it really commercial with a commuter train to Andchestford in the morning with a return journey after work. You perhaps know that my husband, or Mr Hetherington, or Mr Jones, sometimes from pleasure, or because they detest official vandalism, are involved in many good causes, but they've had nothing to do with steam engines. Everybody was shocked when the station was pulled down."

"You get really close to the fields and all the countryside which come right up to the coaches," said Arthur.

"I am very fond of gardening and interested in flowers," said Prunella and added, "I should like to go now, and then again in the spring when the flowers begin to grow. It would be a super idea for the whole family and take my husband completely out of himself, especially as he's had nothing to do with preserving the track."

That lunchtime Prunella and Christopher ate in the Spare Rib Room at The Darlington; so called because of the cheap but adequate meals served there which contrasted with the luxury and opulence of the fare in the rooms further in the interior of the hotel. Donald and Mr Hetherington always had lunch at their homes, but Christopher had always had his at The Darlington because it was too far for him to travel home at midday.

"Arthur has been telling me about steam engines on the

piece of line that has been saved. Not only would you enjoy a visit, especially as there would be nothing to remind you of work, but we could take the children, and keep any leaflets and tickets and perhaps postcards for a school project."

The sequel is brief. Before Christopher could finalize plans with regard to the hotel in Manchester, Jennifer had handed in her notice, and Prunella was never able to dissect Donald because she was too efficient.